Billionaire Unnoticed

THE BILLIONAIRE'S OBSESSION
Cooper

J. S. SCOTT

Billionaire Unnoticed

Copyright © 2021 by J. S. Scott

All rights reserved. No part of this document may be reproduced or transmitted in any form or by any means, electronic, mechanical, photocopying, recording, or otherwise, without prior written permission.

ISBN: 979-8-780799-63-4 (Print)
ISBN: 978-1-951102-49-4 (E-Book)

Contents

Prologue 1
Chapter 1 6
Chapter 2 16
Chapter 3 25
Chapter 4 30
Chapter 5 37
Chapter 6 47
Chapter 7 54
Chapter 8 63
Chapter 9 69
Chapter 10 75
Chapter 11 83
Chapter 12 90
Chapter 13 96
Chapter 14 102
Chapter 15 109
Chapter 16 114
Chapter 17 120
Chapter 18 126
Chapter 19 132

Chapter 20 138
Chapter 21 144
Chapter 22 150
Chapter 23 156
Chapter 24 161
Chapter 25 168
Chapter 26 174
Chapter 27 180
Chapter 28 186
Chapter 29 192
Chapter 30 198
Chapter 31 204
Epilogue 210

Prologue

One Year Earlier…

I knew I had to keep moving even though I was running on empty. Every movement was pure agony. Every second seemed like an hour.

Yet, I *had* to keep going.

I had no other choices.

At this point, it was keep moving…or die.

Crawl, Torie. Keep crawling. You have to get to the river. There's no other way. If you can't get there, you're dead.

I was close enough to hear the flow of the water, but not near enough to be rescued if someone came by on a boat.

I'd be invisible in this jungle.

To be seen, I *had* to get to the riverbank.

So close. I'm so close.

I groaned with pain as I stretched my arm over my head and scooted my body along the forest floor.

My other arm was broken and useless, but that was just one of my many injuries. I hadn't stopped to try to ascertain where all of the blood was coming from that had been slowly oozing from my body.

I knew I didn't have the time or the energy to worry about something I couldn't change right now.

I had to survive.

I needed to be rescued.

The alternative was to die while crawling around in the middle of the Peruvian Amazon jungle, and I'd be damned if I'd give my kidnappers that satisfaction.

I wasn't about to let those bastards win.

Me eventually dying from my injuries was exactly what they'd planned on happening.

My intention was to make sure things didn't work out the way they'd calculated.

Instead of just killing me, they'd beaten me until they'd broken more bones in my body than I could count, and had left me for dead before they'd gone to find a safe hideout.

The assholes had known that someone was going to eventually notice I was missing, and they'd wanted to get as far away as possible.

"Pirates!" I hissed out loud as I kept inching my way toward the Amazon River. "How in the hell could I have known I'd be snatched by pirates?"

The possibility hadn't even been on my radar two weeks ago when I'd been rushing to join my riverboat cruise in Nauta.

Focus, Torie! You have to get to the river.

I knew my chances of rescue were pretty slim, but I had to hang on to some kind of hope.

I lay there for a moment, panting, my face resting against the ground while I tried to get a grip on the pain that was raging through my entire body.

I knew I was badly injured.

That agony radiated through every part of my body,

I was dazed, and I'd lost track of exactly how long I'd been crawling toward the river.

Once my kidnappers had beaten me senseless, I'd lost consciousness for a while. By the time I'd come to, they'd already fled.

I'd understood every word they'd spoken during my two-week ordeal, so I'd been totally aware that they'd left me for dead in a very remote area of the Amazon.

I was a linguist, a woman with a gift for languages, and Spanish was one of the languages I could understand and speak like a native.

Not that I'd been very chatty with the bastards who had nearly killed me, but I'd known from the very beginning that the two men hadn't planned on letting me leave the Amazon alive.

Even though they'd started out with the not-so-brilliant idea of holding me hostage for ransom, me emerging from this remote rainforest alive hadn't *ever* been an option.

Both of the men were pure evil. Torturing and tormenting me had all been an entertaining game for them.

"Assholes," I rasped, my anger urging me forward.

Of course they'd deprived me of food and water, giving just enough to keep me alive. Unfortunately, I'd been weak from deprivation and previous torture well before they'd started to kick the crap out of me.

Afterward, my rage had been the only thing allowing me to move at all.

I'll most likely die of my injuries before anyone finds me.

I immediately rejected that thought and thrust it from my head as I kept struggling to get to the water.

I had to hang on to my anger, my fury, and my outrage. It was the only thing keeping me conscious and advancing forward.

As the sound of flowing water got louder, I stopped crawling and reached to swipe the blood from my eyes.

Move faster, Torie! Get to the river before you pass out or lose the ability to move.

My heart was racing, most likely from my blood loss and the adrenaline flowing through my body.

I. Need. To. Live.

I. Want. To. Live.

A sob escaped from my lips as I kept crawling.

I was barely thirty-one years old.

I hadn't even settled down…yet.

I *hoped* to get married one day.
I *hoped* to have kids.
I *hoped* to be around to see my two older brothers do the same thing.
I wasn't ready to die yet, dammit!
My hand finally slapped down at the top of the riverbank, and I let out a strangled sob of relief.
If I'd had the strength, I would have screamed with agony as I flipped onto my back.
I have to be visible to any passing watercraft.
Using one arm and the leg with the least amount of injuries, I propelled myself slowly down the riverbank until I was right in the middle of the fairly gentle slope.
Completely visible if anyone should pass by via the river.
Okay, so there was a possibility that I could eventually become caiman food if I lay here too long, but by that time I'd probably be dead. I hadn't seen a single caiman in this area on my trip down the river, so I was willing to take my chances.
I closed my eyes as blood from my head wounds started to flow down my face again.
I was done. I couldn't move another inch. I'd done everything I could do to save myself.
I needed medical treatment.
I needed food.
I needed water.
I was close to the latter, but the water of the Amazon River wasn't safe to drink untreated, and I'd already ingested a fair amount accidentally during my captivity.
I knew my survival was now in the hands of fate.
Exhausted, sick, and critically injured, I let my mind wander to a more peaceful place because I couldn't stay grounded in reality anymore.
I relived all of my good memories from my childhood, and I had many of those.

I'd been blessed with an amazing family, including two incredible older brothers who were going to be frantic when they realized I was missing.

A lone tear trickled down my cheek as I recalled every treasured memory of my deceased father and mother before my mind grew hazy.

"I'm sorry," I said in a hoarse, tormented whisper as I saw a vague image of my older brothers, Chase and Wyatt.

Our mother had died of cancer when I was a teenager, but my father's death was more recent and still painful for all of us.

I knew if I died here in this rainforest, my brothers would find some way to blame themselves, and that thought made my heart ache.

My older brothers had always been my protectors, even though they knew I was perfectly capable of taking care of myself.

If something happened to me, I knew it would have a profound effect on both of their lives, and remorse flooded my being right before I lost all ability to think.

Darkness loomed, and I fought it briefly before I finally allowed myself to sink into that welcoming, pain-free oblivion.

There was no reason not to escape the pain anymore since my destiny was no longer in my own hands.

Chapter 1

Cooper

The Present...

"I really need a favor, Coop," my friend, Chase Durand, told me when I answered my cell phone.
No greeting?
No smart-ass comments?
This definitely was not behavior that was typical of Chase.
He continued in a sober tone, "I wouldn't ask, but Wyatt and I are still in Paris. We'll probably have to be here for a few more months. We're trying to move as much of the headquarters as possible back to San Diego so we won't have to be here as long in the future. Neither of us like being away from Last Hope for months at a time. But this extended stay really sucks right now."
The hair stood up at the back of my neck.
Something was wrong.
Chase was rarely this serious. His older brother, Wyatt, tended to be much quieter and more thoughtful, but if Chase *wasn't* joking around, something definitely wasn't right.

Billionaire Unnoticed

"What's up?" I asked.

I'd always trusted Chase to have my back in any situation, and that wasn't something I could say about very many people in my life—other than my own brothers.

If he needed my help because he was out of the country, I was all over whatever that problem might be. He'd do the same for me in a heartbeat.

"Are you home?" he asked.

"Yeah," I confirmed as I headed toward my kitchen. "Just walked through the door, actually. I got out of the office a little early today."

It was Friday, and since I'd been working late all week at the office because Montgomery Mining was opening a new diamond mine, I'd decided to knock off a little early this afternoon. All of the issues with the new mine had been resolved.

I'd planned on changing my clothes and heading toward the dog training center my brother Jax and I supported financially. The dogs that were selected from the shelter were taught to function as assistance dogs for military veterans.

There were currently a couple of intelligent canines there that I took out for a run regularly because they needed to blow off steam.

However, whatever Chase needed right now was going to take priority. My run with the mutts would have to wait.

"It's Torie," Chase explained.

I tensed and held back a tormented groan.

Thirteen days.

Six hours.

Ten Minutes.

And...

I took a glance at my watch.

Exactly twenty-seven seconds.

That was precisely how long it had been since I'd first met Victoria "Torie" Durand, Chase and Wyatt's younger sister.

Fuck! Anything but that! I'd just as soon parachute out of a plane at high altitude and into shark-infested waters than to deal with any kind of issue for Chase that involved his little sister, Torie Durand.

It wasn't that I didn't like Torie…exactly. Truth was, since the moment we'd met almost two weeks ago, I'd tried really hard to avoid her.

She was wickedly smart, a talented linguist who spoke and wrote more languages than any single person should be capable of translating.

She was also strikingly beautiful.

And, for some damn reason, I'd felt some kind of weird connection to her since the moment we'd met, which I *logically* knew was impossible.

I was pragmatic.

I was not in the least idealistic.

I didn't believe in soul mates or having an affinity with another person I'd just met.

It wasn't…rational.

There was no such thing as an instant connection with another person, for fuck's sake.

The thought was pure fantasy.

So, yeah, I *could* ignore that weird sense of affinity I'd mistakenly thought I'd felt that couldn't possibly exist.

What I *couldn't* overlook was the very real fact that my dick got rock-hard every time we were in the same space together.

I couldn't see her—or even think about her—without wanting to get her naked.

Quite honestly, I wasn't sure how to handle a physical attraction that fierce since it had never happened quite that way for me before.

So yeah, Victoria Durand was trouble. I'd learned to steer clear of anything or anyone that might interfere with my vow to stay romantically unentangled.

That shit had never worked out well for me.

Over the last year, I hadn't even been tempted to change my mind about dating…until Torie Durand.

Damned if she didn't make me want to reconsider my stance on relationships—which made her extremely dangerous to me.

That's why I avoided her.

I was better off alone.

I didn't need a romantic relationship in my life…again. Not after the last one had worked out particularly bad.

Before I could draw a breath to tell Chase I'd send one of my brothers to help him out, he continued. "I called Torie earlier. She went for a hike this afternoon at Mission Trails Park. She supposedly *tweaked* her ankle, whatever the hell *that* means. She claims that she's fine, and she's walking out of the park, but she joked that her progress was going to be slow. It's likely to be dark before she makes it back to the parking lot. I don't like it, Coop. She's a really experienced hiker, and I get that it's an urban park where you're never that far from the city, but she's still an injured female in eight thousand acres of undeveloped land. She's alone, Coop. I hate the thought of her being that vulnerable."

Fuck! There was an edgy desperation in Chase's tone that I'd never heard before. Unfortunately, his uneasiness immediately sparked the same discomfort inside of me.

My jaw twitched as I yanked a backpack out of a closet near the front door. I took it with me back to the kitchen and started to toss some supplies into it.

There was no way in hell I *wasn't* going after Torie myself at this point. There was no time for someone else to do it. I wasn't waiting until I could get in touch with one of my older brothers.

Yeah, there were probably others on the trails today. It was a popular park in the cooler, winter weather because it had very little shade in the summer. But those visitors weren't going to help Torie since she didn't know any of them. In fact, it was those other people at the park who concerned me.

She was alone.

She was hurt, which made her prey to anyone with nefarious intentions.

And knowing she had no one around to watch out for her when she was almost defenseless bothered me more than the fact that my dick got hard every time I saw her.

I took a quick glance at my watch.

It was after three o'clock. Since we were just barely into January, the sun would set by five.

Some of those trails could be a little rocky and uneven for someone with an ankle injury.

Hell, Chase was right. There was no way she *wasn't* going to lose the light before she could get out of the park. Did she even have a headlamp or a flashlight with her?

"What supplies does she have? How far is she from the parking lot?" I asked tersely as I sprinted up the stairs to get a sweatshirt.

"Next to nothing," Chase answered, his voice irritated. "This wasn't supposed to be an overnighter or an evening hike. It was more like a…longish midafternoon walk for Torie. She said she'd planned on being home before it was even close to dark. It looks to me like she was about three miles from her vehicle when I talked to her, which wouldn't be a big deal if she *wasn't* injured. She sounded like she was hurting, Coop. She says everything is fine, but I'd feel a hell of a lot better if I was there to walk out with her. She might need someone to look at that ankle."

"I'm on it," I assured him. "Do you think we should alert the rangers?"

"Already done," Chase informed me. "They weren't particularly concerned since she's not exactly missing, and she's not requesting medical assistance. Her intention is to leave the park on her own two feet. Hell, maybe I'm overreacting because—"

"You're not," I grumbled. "If this was happening to Riley, I'd be worried, too." I'd go after my younger sister in a heartbeat if she were in the same situation, so I could relate to Chase's frustration. "I'll be out of here and on my way in a few minutes. It will probably take me twenty minutes to get there. Do you have coordinates of where she's at right now?"

My waterfront home in La Jolla wasn't that far from where Torie was located, but it was after three on a Friday. Traffic was going to suck.

"She's on the move," Chase replied. "But I'll send you the map of the trail she's on and what her coordinates were when I talked to her on the phone. I have a feeling she hasn't gotten very far."

"That works," I told him as I raced back down the stairs to the kitchen again. "I know that park pretty well." I'd gone running there plenty of times, so none of the trails were unfamiliar to me. I just needed Torie's general location to find her since there were several trails she could be following.

"She's trying to pretend like she's all right," Chase grumbled. "But she's not. I think she's just trying not to worry me, but it's not fucking working. I can hear the pain in her voice—no matter how well she tries to hide it. She might be moving, but I can tell that every step is killing her."

My heart sank.

Shit!

I really didn't like thinking about Torie in any kind of pain, either.

"Why is she out there alone? Doesn't she have hiking buddies?" I questioned Chase.

"Torie likes to do solo trips sometimes to clear her head, but it's actually been quite a while since she's been out on any trail," he explained.

"I'll find her," I promised Chase. "And I'll get her injury checked out."

"Thanks, man," Chase replied, sounding relieved. "Torie won't be happy that I sent someone to check on her after she told me she was okay."

I finally hefted the pack over my shoulder and reached for the keys to my Range Rover. "I'll do my best not to make it obvious that you sent me," I told him.

"She'll know," Chase said unhappily. "Her intuition is scary. I doubt she'll believe it's a coincidence that you just happened to show up in that park."

"You're probably right," I agreed. "She seems too damn smart to buy that, but I'll do my best."

"So you two have obviously met now that she's volunteering at Last Hope," Chase surmised.

I dropped my pack into the passenger seat and got into my vehicle. "We have," I answered, hoping he wouldn't ask more questions.

Chase and Wyatt had arrived in Europe a month or so before Torie had decided to join Last Hope, a volunteer private rescue organization that we all belonged to now.

Until very recently, Last Hope had consisted solely of guys who were previous special forces members. We took on foreign rescue operations that the government wouldn't touch.

Torie and my brother Jax's girlfriend, Harlow, had been the first two women to join the secret organization because we'd needed the services they were offering.

Harlow was a weather specialist.

Torie was a linguist.

My first meeting with Torie had happened at Last Hope headquarters in downtown San Diego nearly two weeks ago.

I'd done my best to avoid her at headquarters ever since.

It wasn't like we hung out together, but yeah, we'd…met.

"I always assumed you two would get along," Chase mused.

"Why?" I questioned dryly as I got on the freeway. "Just because our IQs are both so high that it makes us freaks of nature."

Torie was intellectually gifted, just like I was, but her talents obviously leaned more toward the languages, while mine were more generalized in reasoning abilities and logic.

"It's not *just* that," Chase replied, ignoring my sarcasm. "You two actually have a lot in common. Torie likes the outdoors. You're both hikers, and she shares your love of reading and history. Although I have to admit that you're both so stubborn that you might just end up clashing."

"I'm not stubborn," I grumbled.

Chase chuckled. "Says the man who hasn't gotten laid in over a year because his girlfriend was stupid enough to dump him so she could marry an idiot."

I wasn't even going to argue about his assumption since it was true. For the most part, anyway. "Fuck off, Durand. You know nothing about my sex life."

And even if he *did* know that I was having a long dry spell, I doubted very much that he'd want Torie to be the woman who fixed *that* particular problem.

No doubt Chase had hoped that Torie and I would become friends, not lovers.

"I'll let you get away with telling me to fuck off since you're helping me out," Chase answered with a chuckle. "How are things going at Last Hope? We've been an all-male organization for so long that it has to be strange to have women at the headquarters."

"Having Harlow and Torie on board helps a lot," I admitted reluctantly. "It's great as long as the two of them stay safe," I replied. "It's not the fact that they're female that concerns me. It's their lack of experience in rescue situations. Both Harlow and Torie have incredibly valuable skills, but I don't want to see either one of them in a situation they aren't trained to handle."

"They won't be," Chase assured me. "We'll all be watching out for both of them, and they're perfectly safe at headquarters. The place is harder to get into than Fort Knox. Neither one of them will ever be present on missions. Fuck knows that Jax isn't about to see Harlow do anything that might harm a hair on her head."

"No, he definitely won't," I agreed. My brother practically lost his shit if his girlfriend got a hangnail. Not that I didn't understand that—to a point—since Harlow had been a captive and put through hell and back during that kidnapping. Jax would give up his own life before he'd see Harlow in any kind of danger.

The same with my brother Hudson when it came to his fiancée, Taylor, the second victim in the same kidnapping as Harlow's.

I shook my head as I got onto the freeway.

My two older brothers were completely screwed when it came to the women in their lives.

Honestly, I never thought I'd ever see Hudson or Jax fall so hard, but the two of them were thoroughly lost. Furthermore, they didn't seem to give a damn if they never found their way back to sanity again.

It wasn't that I didn't like Taylor and Harlow. Honestly, I couldn't have asked for two better women for my older brothers.

I just wished Jax and Hudson weren't so damn…obsessive and irrational when it came to Taylor and Harlow.

Love had made both of them lose their minds, but they were such happy lunatics that it was hard *not* to be glad for both of them. Hell, if spending the rest of their lives half insane was what they really wanted, I wasn't going to keep reminding them that they were completely illogical when it came to the women in their lives.

"Since we rarely get out in the field anymore, we'll all take turns making sure they're safe while they're helping out at headquarters," Chase told me earnestly.

"Do you ever miss it?" I asked Chase before I could stop myself.

"What?"

"Doing the missions ourselves?"

Since Hudson, Jax, and I had pretty recognizable faces, we'd stopped running the actual rescue missions ourselves a few years ago.

Even though we avoided the press as much as possible, three billionaire brothers had a very hard time dodging the media all the time.

Wyatt and Chase had quit going into the field for the same reasons.

We'd known that if anyone recognized our faces, even our victims, that Last Hope would lose that edge of secrecy that had helped us be so successful with so many missions over the years.

It wasn't like our skills at strategically planning the missions weren't important, but sometimes it sucked to hand over a planned op to someone else to carry out. It definitely wasn't something any of us had done when we'd been active duty in special forces.

Sometimes, handing those missions over to someone else to execute still felt unnatural, even though we knew it was necessary, and we'd been doing it for years now.

"I do miss it," Chase confessed in a low, thoughtful voice. "But I have to have faith in the men we've taken on as volunteers. I don't want my identity to jeopardize any current or future rescue operations."

"Yeah," I agreed. "Last Hope is the last organization of its kind, so I'm willing to do almost anything to make sure we're not outed."

"I'm not gonna lie," Chase confessed. "There have been plenty of times I've wished I could tag along instead of executing everything from headquarters."

"Me, too," I admitted.

Chase chuckled. "We need that brain of yours at headquarters, Coop. You're a lot more valuable in mission problem solving at headquarters than you are in the field." He hesitated for a moment before he added gruffly, "Thanks for doing this for me."

"It's not a big deal," I said, meaning every word.

What Chase was asking me to do was a small favor.

The only thing making it difficult was how badly I wanted to get Torie Durand naked.

I kept my mouth shut. My difficulty keeping my dick under control when I saw Torie wasn't an issue I ever planned on sharing with her older brother.

Chapter 2

Torie

A little more than two miles.
I've got this.
It's not all that far to get back to my vehicle.
"God, I'm so full of shit," I mumbled. Every damn step felt like a mile, and two more miles was going to feel like fifty in the condition I was in right now.

I winced as I kept putting one foot in front of the other at a snail's pace. *Shit! Shit! Shit!*

I'd walked this hiking route dozens of times when I was younger, and it had never been *this* painful before.

It had also never taken this damn long to hobble back to the parking lot, either.

I sighed and took the last few sips of my water before placing the empty bottle back into a small day pack.

I was still thirsty, but I wasn't about to fall over from heat exhaustion.

In fact, even though the day had been pleasantly warm for January, it was starting to cool off now that the sun was getting lower.

I tried to console myself with the thought that the rest of the walk wasn't too horrible. At least I was beyond the massive stairway on this particular trail. The terrain was a little rough in a few places, but the worst of the trail was over.

What in the hell had I been thinking when I'd scrambled over that stupid boulder?

It wasn't like I'd *had* to get over it.

It wasn't in the middle of the trail.

I'd just wanted a better vantage point, so I'd scrambled up, and hadn't been careful enough when I'd decided to hop back down.

Dammit! It wasn't like I didn't know better than to get too cocky on any hike, even one I'd done dozens of times here in San Diego before I'd gone off to college.

Not to mention the fact that I hadn't been out on *any* trail in over a year, so most of my hiking skills were rusty.

That should have made me extra careful, right?

Nope. It hadn't. I'd managed to tweak my ankle on my first time out in ages on a fairly easy hike.

I grimaced as I tried to pick up my pace, knowing if I didn't start to hustle, I was going to end up out on this trail after dark.

I tried not to allow panic to start taking over my brain at the thought of being alone in the dark.

I was pretty much over that, right?

I'd done plenty of nighttime walks to desensitize myself, but somehow, being alone *and injured* felt slightly…different.

You'll be fine, Torie. Just keep moving. Keep focused on getting to the parking lot right now.

Since it was getting late and it did get dark pretty damn early this time of year, I wasn't really encountering many other hikers on the trail, which was fine with me.

I felt like a total idiot, and the fewer people who witnessed my humiliation, the better.

I'd done some of the most hardcore hikes in the world, and here I was hobbling out of an urban regional park in San Diego like a damned novice.

Worse yet, I'd worried my brother, and I hated that.

I'd put Chase and Wyatt through enough over the last year or so. Not that either one of them had complained. They'd simply delayed going to Paris until they felt comfortable leaving me alone in San Diego.

I sighed as I forced myself to keep moving. I'd traveled to Paris to spend Christmas with my brothers, but I still missed them.

I probably shouldn't have answered my cell phone when Chase had called earlier, but I'd been so damn miserable that I'd wanted to talk to someone.

Unfortunately, I sucked at trying to hide anything from my brothers.

Chase had recognized the fact that I was uncomfortable, and he'd nagged the hell out of me until I told him that I'd tweaked my ankle out here.

I'll call him once I get to the car, let him know I'm okay.

I'd promised Chase he'd get a call the second I was in my vehicle, so the sooner I got there, the better.

I pushed on, resigning myself to the fact that I probably wasn't going to get out of the park by nightfall.

There was just no possible way I could move fast enough to be in my car by the time it got dark.

Beyond the fact that I still had a few irrational fears of being alone in the dark, there were other reasons I didn't want to be out here once the sun had set.

Yeah, I had the flashlight on my phone, so I had something I could use if I couldn't see the trail, but I wasn't exactly prepared for a night hike, and didn't have the equipment I needed—even if I'd wanted to hike in the dark.

Although this was a regional park in San Diego, there were coyotes, mountain lions, and other nocturnal wildlife I'd prefer not to encounter today.

I sure as hell won't be able to run or get away. Almost any animal out here—except for maybe a turtle—is faster than I am right now.

I was so busy watching my step and wallowing in my pity party for one that I never noticed when someone else started keeping pace right beside me.

"You really don't look like you're enjoying this particular hike," Cooper Montgomery commented as he casually strolled along next to me with his hands in his pockets.

My eyes shot up to his face and I stopped abruptly in the middle of the trail.

I bit back a groan.

Dammit!

If there was one single person on Earth I *didn't* want to talk to right now, it was Cooper. "What are you doing here?"

He shrugged. "Just out for a little hike, same as you."

I snorted. "You're a lousy liar. What you really mean is that my brother Chase called you because he was worried about me."

Really? Did he honestly think I'd fall for the I-just-happen-to-be-out-walking-in-this-park-too bullshit?

I had to force back a sigh as I took in his appearance.

God, he looked amazing in a long-sleeved, navy-blue Henley, jeans, and a pair of hiking boots.

He hadn't even worked up a sweat.

Cooper's physical appearance was annoyingly perfect. He kept his blond hair clipped fairly short and it was always so neatly groomed that I was tempted to spear a hand into his hair and mess it all up a little. Just so he wasn't quite so stunningly flawless.

Problem was, I had no doubt that a disheveled, just-rolled-out-of-bed look would probably be even more appealing on him.

Cooper had a pair of unusual, piercing, light blue eyes that appeared to look almost like they were lightly brushed with frost. Maybe that particular color should have made his eyes look bitterly cold, but strangely, it didn't.

His tall, muscular body was honed like it belonged to a guy who pushed himself to his physical limits. Cooper was tall and ridiculously muscular, just the type of guy who I could easily find intimidating, but for some reason, I never had.

He frowned at me. "Is it that unbelievable that I just happened to be out for a hike? It actually is one of my hobbies. And I've also used this park to do daily runs more times than I can count."

I nearly snorted. I could buy that he took some runs here, but the idea that he walked or hiked here was ludicrous. There would be zero challenge for him on these paths.

I nodded. "The whole idea *is* absolutely unbelievable. You'd never hike here, and it would be totally illogical to believe in a coincidence this big. Plus, I know my brother. He's worried, and since he can't be here, it's logical for him to send someone who he considers the next best thing to being here himself."

In my mind, sending in a guy to rescue me who was previous Army Green Beret who packed a Glock at all times was probably overkill, but I doubted Chase thought the same way.

Cooper didn't confirm or deny before he instructed, "Sit down on that big rock over there. I want to look at your ankle."

"No need," I assured him nervously. "It's not broken. I'm walking on it."

Sure, I found Cooper attractive aesthetically, but I was still a little uncomfortable about being touched by a man I didn't know.

"Humor me," he insisted in a no-nonsense baritone.

I doubted that I was going to get rid of him until I did as he requested, so I sat. I was too disheartened to do anything else. "I'm not sure how easy it will be to get my boot back on after you're done looking at this ankle."

My ankle had swelled nearly to the size of a grapefruit, and once it was out of the boot, I wasn't confident it would go back in again.

"Not a problem," he answered gruffly as he squatted down and untied the laces on the hiking boot and started gingerly pulling it off my foot. "Christ! Your ankle really is swollen."

Hadn't I just told him that?

I flinched as he gently tugged my boot completely off. Not because Cooper was touching me, but because it freaking hurt. "It's worse than it was a mile ago," I admitted as I examined my ankle with a frown.

He looked up at me and quirked a brow. "You think? That's what usually happens when you put additional stress on an already injured ankle."

"It's not like I had much choice unless I wanted to spend the night here," I snipped.

Crap! I got that Cooper had one of highest IQs in the world, but I wasn't a complete idiot.

I let out an exasperated breath. While I really appreciated the fact that he had responded when Chase had asked him to come check on my progress, I wasn't in the mood for a lecture.

Especially when that censure was coming from Cooper Montgomery.

I doubted very much whether a guy as smart as Cooper would make such a stupid mistake.

He was ridiculously…perfect.

And for some reason I couldn't explain, his opinion…mattered to me.

Hell, I'd rather Chase had sent a complete stranger that I'd never have to see again.

"I don't have as much medical training as Jax does," Cooper said as he palpated my ankle. "But I think you're right. I don't think it's broken, but you definitely tore a ligament. It's bruising. That usually means there's some bleeding into the tissues from the torn ligament. You can't keep walking on this, Torie. It may not be broken, but it's a bad sprain."

I watched, fascinated as he expertly wrapped a small icepack around the ankle and then secured it so it wouldn't be falling off anytime soon.

He was confident and capable, even when he was doing something he probably hadn't done in quite a while.

Cooper shoved my hiking boot into his backpack when he was finished wrapping my ankle.

"I think I'm going to need that," I told him, confused by his actions.

He shook his head as he removed his Glock from his waistband, checked the safety, and added it into his backpack. "No, you won't."

Okay, so maybe Cooper was a man of few words, but he was going to need to explain how I was going to traverse the rocky terrain without something on my foot.

"You'll have to handle my pack," he said as he pulled a bottle of ice-cold water from his backpack and handed it to me. "Drink some of that before we take off. You look tired, possibly thirsty, and overall like you're completely done with this entire expedition today."

I was all three of those things, and his water tasted so damn good. What little water I'd had left for this long return journey hadn't exactly been cold.

"Put this on when you're done," he rumbled as he passed me a sweatshirt from his pack. "It's going to get cooler now that the sun is going down and you won't be moving around much."

Again, I didn't argue because I *was* a little cold. I was wearing a pair of jeans, but my top was fairly thin and short-sleeved.

It would make absolutely no sense to quibble about something I wanted, even though his commands might be slightly high-handed.

The moment I had the garment on, I knew it had to be Cooper's. Even though I was far from tiny, I was practically swimming in the sweatshirt.

Once everything was back into the pack, he zipped it and slung it over my shoulder. Then he turned around, and bent down as he said, "Jump on."

What? He didn't seriously think that…

I frowned. Letting him bandage up my ankle was one thing, but climbing onto his back and literally riding him to the parking lot was another.

"Cooper, you can't possibly piggyback me for two miles," I insisted. "You're a big, strong guy, but that's just crazy. I'm not exactly a delicate featherweight."

"I've lugged a lot heavier weights for several miles," he said with a touch of humor in his voice. "I'm perfectly capable, Torie. Hop on. We're starting to lose a lot of daylight."

Just the thought of giving my painful ankle a break was so damn tempting.

Maybe I can let him haul me around…just for a little while? Maybe I can handle it since I'll be on his back?

It would definitely help both of us get back to the parking lot faster.

Before I could stop to think about it long enough to change my mind, I wrapped my arms around his neck and hitched my legs around his waist.

It was a shock to my system as he straightened because we were in such an intimate position. Especially after he put a hand underneath both my thighs to stabilize me. "You tell me the second you get tired and I'll walk," I said insistently.

I could almost see his smirk as he answered, "Yep. You'll know the second you get to be too much for me."

Arrogant smart-ass!

Once I was settled, Cooper began to eat up the distance with long, powerful strides. The guy was as surefooted as a mountain goat on the rocky terrain.

Embarrassed, I tried to lighten my death grip around his neck.

If he was going to sprint me back to the parking lot, the least I could do was let the poor guy breathe.

"I'm sorry you ended up being the poor soul that Chase called to help me," I said glumly. "I would have eventually made it out of the park. If I really needed help, I could have called the park rangers."

"Don't," Cooper answered huskily.

"Don't what?" I asked.

"Don't blame Chase. He was worried. He's your brother. I'm not sorry that he called me, Torie," he said in a genuine tone of voice.

I sucked in a deep breath and couldn't quite hold back a small moan as I savored Cooper's earthy, masculine scent.

We were too damn close.

Too intimate.

And it was absolutely impossible to put any distance between the two of us right now.

Strangely, the edginess I was feeling had nothing to do with fear and everything to do with my female hormones.

Although it was unexpected for me to feel this way, it wasn't completely surprising.

It had been like this with Cooper Montgomery since the moment we'd met.

Well, for me, anyway.

I definitely wasn't the kind of woman who swooned over a pretty face and a hot body, but there was something about this man that… drew me to him.

Unfortunately, that fascination definitely didn't go both ways.

"You okay back there?" Cooper asked, sounding concerned.

"Fine," I squeaked. "It's just a relief to be off my ankle."

Honestly, my biggest problem at the moment was trying to stop my overwhelming attraction to my rescuer.

I'd finally found a man that didn't make me shiver with revulsion when he touched me, but why did that particular male have to be Cooper Montgomery?

I lowered my forehead gently to his shoulder, closed my eyes, and tried not to hate myself for lusting after a guy who had no desire to do anything except help me out of a bad situation right now.

Chapter 3

Cooper

What kind of asshole thought about having sex with a woman who was in pain and barely able to walk? *Fuck! What the hell is wrong with me?*

Torie's ankle was messed up and swollen so badly that she didn't have a hope in hell of getting that hiking boot on again anytime soon.

Still, with her legs wrapped around me, and that gorgeous body of hers plastered to my back, all I could think about was being this close to her under far more…erotic circumstances.

I gritted my teeth and forced those desires out of my head.

She *was* injured.

She *was* in pain.

She *did* need my help right now.

Her body *was not* clinging to mine by choice, and suddenly remembering *that* helped me escape from my lurid thoughts about Torie.

Well, for the most part, anyway.

Unfortunately, I'd probably remember her unique, sensual scent well after she was off my back and miles away.

"Shit! I'm such a twisted bastard," I muttered angrily under my breath.

"Did you say something?" Torie asked softly, right next to my ear.

"No," I lied without a single twinge of guilt. "Nothing important."

"Cooper, you've already covered a lot of ground. You're going to have to let me walk sooner or later," she insisted.

"Not happening," I informed her. "Your ankle is a mess, and you're not exactly heavy. Do you have any idea what kind of physical hell they put us through in special forces?"

"But you're not in special forces anymore. You haven't been for years," she reminded me.

"I stay fit," I told her.

Habits were hard to break. Maybe it had been years since I'd gone from the 75th Ranger Unit to the Green Berets. But fitness had always remained part of my life.

"That's pretty obvious," she said in a breathless voice. "But my brothers always say they can never stay as fit as they were while they were in the military."

"They're right. None of us are living the same life we were in the military. We were constantly active then. Now, we all sit in an office for way too much of our days. Luckily, carrying you for a few miles doesn't require that active duty level of fitness," I told her honestly.

"I think you're absolutely insane," Torie answered. "But thank you for this. I know I didn't greet you very graciously after you came all the way here just to help me out. I guess I was just…embarrassed, but I know I wouldn't have gotten out of this myself until way after nightfall, so I don't want you to think that I'm not grateful."

She's…grateful?

Hell, the last thing I really wanted was Torie's gratitude.

I took a few careful steps over some jagged rocks and resumed my previous pace. I was determined to get Torie out of here before it was completely dark.

"You have no reason to be embarrassed," I told her calmly. "Accidents happen when we're challenging our skills sometimes."

"That's just it," she said mournfully. "This wasn't a challenge, Cooper. It was a dumb mistake. I've hiked some of the most difficult trails in the country, including The Maze in Utah, and South Kaibab Trail in the Grand Canyon. I'm not a novice, and I feel like an idiot because I got careless on a familiar route like this one. I probably hiked this trail a thousand times as a teenager, and this park hasn't changed much. It's been here for decades. I hopped down from a boulder and turned my ankle at a regional park in my hometown. How idiotic is that?"

Okay, I was impressed. I'd never had a chance to do The Maze myself, but from what I understood, it was one of the most difficult hikes in the country. No one even attempted it unless they were an expert hiker. There was an entire labyrinth of trails that led to many dead-end canyons. It was also difficult because the interconnecting canyons all looked the same, the high cliffs had no vantage points, water supplies were scarce, and temperatures could reach one hundred and eighteen degrees in the summer. One mistake and a hiker could end up stranded if they could make it until someone rescued them. Or dead if they couldn't.

I had done the South Kaibab Trail, and it was no joke. It was a long, tough, steep hike with limited water supplies and scorching temperatures.

My respect for Torie's skills went up several notches.

"Sometimes, when we're more relaxed, we slip up," I told her. "It happens, Torie. It's human nature to let your guard down a little in a familiar place. Don't beat yourself up over it."

"Normally, I probably wouldn't," she explained. "But you're so…"

Oh, hell no. She couldn't stop there. "I'm so…what?" I prompted.

"You're so damn…perfect," she said with a sigh. "And you've made it pretty clear that you don't like me, so this situation is even more demoralizing."

"Wait a minute. I'm far from perfect," I said as I hopped over a couple of large rocks. "And who said I didn't like you?"

"Come on, Cooper. It's obvious that you avoid me. We haven't spoken since the day we met two weeks ago. If I'm walking toward you at Last Hope headquarters, you practically sprint in a different direction. I'm not sure what I ever did to make you dislike me—"

"You didn't do anything," I interrupted. "It has nothing to do with you."

It had never occurred to me that Torie had actually noticed that I went out of my way to avoid her. Or that it might hurt her feelings if she had.

"I don't understand," she answered, sounding confused. "When we first met, I thought that we might become friends. We both grew up a little bit different because we're intellectually gifted, and even though you pulled that stupid gun on me the first time we met, I still liked you and wanted to get to know you."

I could honestly say no one had ever called my Glock *a stupid gun* before, but she was right. Our first meeting hadn't exactly been ideal.

I'd arrived at headquarters late one night, only to hear someone prowling around upstairs.

So yeah, I'd pulled my gun since I'd known the location of everyone who worked at headquarters, and none of them were supposed to be in the building that evening.

At the time, I hadn't yet discovered that Marshall, the leader of Last Hope, had accepted Torie's offer of volunteering her linguist services.

Hell, I hadn't even known she'd offered them or that Chase and Wyatt's sister had even known about Last Hope's existence.

Finding Torie in one of the upstairs offices had been a surprise that had knocked me off my game.

I'd been momentarily stunned, but I'd pulled out of my stupor fairly quickly.

No matter how transfixed I'd been with Torie's beautiful amber eyes, her seemingly endless waves of light brown hair, and her curvy body, I'd harshly reminded myself that I didn't do long-term relationships.

Not anymore.

And since she was the younger sister of two men I highly respected, there was no way I was going to act on my physical attraction to her.

"I don't dislike you, Torie. I hardly know you, and anything I've ever heard about you from Chase and Wyatt was nothing but praise," I told her earnestly.

"You'd get to know me a whole lot better if you didn't run away from me like your ass was on fire," she told me good-naturedly. "Maybe we'd actually have a chance to be friends or at least have some kind of conversation."

"I doubt that's going to happen," I replied solemnly.

"Why not?" she questioned, her voice sounding like I'd just slapped her.

Fuck! I hate that. I obviously hurt her feelings…again.

But did I have any options except honestly?

I kept surveying our surroundings until I finally saw the parking lot in the distance. "I'm not looking for a relationship, Torie, friends or otherwise."

What I'd really meant was that I couldn't possibly be around her without wanting to get her naked, but I wasn't about to tell her that. I'd rather sound like a major prick than a pathetic loser.

She sighed. "I'm no more eager to have a romantic relationship than you are right now, Cooper. They've never worked out any better for me than they have for you, and I've been out of the dating scene for well over a year now."

I had no idea why, but the idea of Torie being as cynical as I was about love and relationships somehow…bothered me. "Don't give up," I told her gruffly.

"I'm not," she assured me. "Not really. I've just been…taking a break."

My gut instinct was screaming that there was more to Torie's story than she was admitting.

That slight hesitance had been telling, but I wasn't about to pursue her reasons for shying away from a relationship.

It was none of my business.

It wasn't like I could ever apply for her vacant *significant other* position, so I decided that it was probably safer not to ask any questions at all.

Chapter 4

Torie

"You do realize that when you stopped to pick up dinner, you took all my preconceived ideas about you and blew them all straight to hell, right?" I asked Cooper as we demolished our Double-Double Cheeseburgers, fries, and shakes from In-N-Out Burger at my condo later that evening. "I never pegged you as a junk food kind of guy. Not that I'm complaining."

In-N-Out was one of my favorite fast food places to indulge. I'd been more than willing to pick up something to eat there when Cooper had suggested it right after we left the hospital.

As the evening had worn on I'd gotten more and more comfortable in Cooper's presence.

Granted, he wasn't exactly talkative most of the time, but there was something about his quiet stability that had gotten me to unwind and relax.

Cooper had insisted that I get my ankle checked out and X-rayed, and Chase had seconded that opinion.

In the end, it had been the sensible thing to do.

My grade 2 ankle sprain was now elevated on top of a pillow as I sprawled out on my couch in my living room. Cooper had placed an ice pack on top of it to try to take down more of the swelling.

He'd taken a seat in the recliner across from me once he'd sorted out our food.

He raised a brow. "What does a junk food kind of guy look like?"

I wanted to tell him that in my mind, they probably didn't have a body like a god and an ass that could bounce a quarter farther away than I'd be willing to go to retrieve it.

But…I couldn't say *that*, so I settled with replying, "I guess I just assumed that you were probably a health food nut since you keep yourself in such good shape."

Good shape was probably putting it mildly. Any guy who could piggyback a woman of average size and weight for two miles at a rapid pace and hardly break a sweat was ridiculously fit.

He shrugged as he chewed and swallowed. "I like food too much to eat lean meat, fish, and vegetables every night. I'm not exactly fond of protein shakes, either. I don't need a booster to get enough protein and a lot of them are filled with sugar. I try to eat healthy most of the time, but I'm never going to give up a good burger, pizza, or mac-n-cheese."

"Me, either," I said with a sigh.

"I'm not sure why you're surprised," he added. "It's not like your brothers aren't exactly the same way. We've devoured plenty of beer and pizza at Last Hope headquarters after we've had to stay there late for a planning session or a mission. Do you really think I'd be downing a protein shake while they were scarfing down extra-large pizzas with the works? Hell, I have to fight them for my fair share. I'm not about to give it away."

I snorted with amusement because that was exactly what my older brothers would be ordering for a late-night snack. "I suppose not. Since you and my brothers are close, I should have known you had some of the same eating habits."

Really, what did I know about Cooper Montgomery except for what my brothers had told me over the last few years, which wasn't much? Because they'd never mentioned a word about Last Hope in the past, they hadn't revealed anything about how they knew Hudson, Jax, and Cooper Montgomery. I'd just known that they were all friends.

Cooper dropped the empty wrapper for his burger into the bag sitting on the coffee table. "I should probably go soon," he said, sounding a little uncomfortable. "Are you going to be okay here alone?"

I rolled my eyes. "I'm not disabled, Cooper. I have a sprained ankle and some injured pride. I'll be fine."

If he didn't want to be here, I wasn't going to force him to stay any longer. I was perfectly capable of taking care of myself.

He eyed me doubtfully. "You're supposed to stay off that ankle for a while. It's really swollen, and it needs to heal. If you try doing too much, too soon, you could make it worse. I left the ibuprofen here on the table so you could take another dose before you go to bed. I'll be back tomorrow to check on you. You have to take it easy until the swelling goes down and your ankle is on the mend."

My heart squeezed inside my chest as I remembered how thoughtful he'd been all evening.

Once he'd gotten me into his Range Rover, he'd taken me directly to the hospital while I called Chase to let him know I was okay.

Cooper had waited patiently, like he had nothing better to do, while they'd done an X-ray and the doctor had done her evaluation in the Emergency Room.

He'd fed me.

He'd arranged to get my vehicle back home for me.

He'd brought me home.

He'd insisted on piggybacking me up to my high-rise condo and settling me on the couch so I'd be comfortable to eat.

How many guys who weren't interested in getting laid or in any kind of relationship were that damn thoughtful?

"Thank you for everything," I said softly as I crumpled up my empty wrappers, leaned forward and tossed them into the bag on the table between us. "You hardly know me, but you gave up your entire Friday night to help me."

"It's not like I had exciting plans," he said drily.

"What did you have planned?" I asked curiously, wondering what a guy like Cooper did on a Friday night.

Maybe he wasn't into committed relationships with women, but a guy who looked like him definitely got laid on a regular basis, right?

Not only was he drop-dead gorgeous, but a wealthy billionaire, too. Cooper co-owned the biggest mining operation in the world with his two older brothers.

"I'd just gotten home from the office when Chase called me," he answered. "I was planning on taking a few of the dogs we have at the training center for a run, and then grabbing some dinner."

"What training center?" I questioned.

I was stunned as he explained that he and his brother Jax funded a training center for assistance dogs that helped veterans with PTSD and other issues.

I was even more surprised when he told me that he and his brother not only paid for the running of the facility, but participated personally in the training when they could as well.

"We adopt the dogs from shelters when we can," he said. "Jax has two of those shelter dogs that he just couldn't part with, but I've managed to not get quite that attached."

I studied his body language and the guarded look in his beautiful eyes.

I was willing to bet that there were plenty of times when Cooper had gotten attached.

He just didn't want anyone to know it.

Any man who was kind and patient enough to work with animals had definitely developed an affinity with those shelter dogs.

I just couldn't figure out exactly why Cooper didn't want to admit it.

What was it with this guy and his aversion to relationships of any kind?

There was an inherent goodness and humanity inside of Cooper. I could see it. I could sense it. Hell, if I needed proof then he'd proved it by coming to rescue me without a single complaint, but for some reason, it seemed like he was determined to hide it beneath cynicism and doubt most of the time.

When I'd thanked him, he'd blown me off—like giving up his evening was next to nothing.

It wasn't.

Cooper Montgomery was one of the wealthiest and most powerful men on the planet. Giving up his precious free time was…really something.

I smiled at him. "Then I did take you away from some important canine friends."

"Chase was concerned," Cooper replied.

I rolled my eyes. "Both of my brothers think that worrying about me is their job, even though I'm thirty-two years old now."

"Most older brothers feel that way. I have a younger sister. I know exactly how they feel," he informed me. "And I'm not quite sure they don't have a reason to worry. You have a pretty long list of past injuries in your medical history for someone your age."

I was stunned into silence for a moment.

Since Cooper had refused to leave my side at the hospital, he'd been privy to my conversations with the doctor. Since I had nothing to hide, I'd told him it was fine for him to stay.

Now, I wasn't quite so sure that had been such a great idea since he'd obviously paid close attention to what was going on.

I swallowed a mouthful of my strawberry shake before I replied. "Most of them were from the same incident that happened a year ago. My injuries were pretty extensive. I'm honestly not *that* accident prone."

"What happened?" he asked huskily.

"Long story," I confessed.

It was a painful episode in my life that I hadn't willingly shared with anyone except my brothers and my best friend…until now.

He lifted a brow. "It's early. I have time."

I wanted to remind him that he'd just mentioned leaving a few minutes ago, but I didn't. Granted, I didn't like talking about what had happened, but Cooper had helped me out so much today. "Before I came back home to San Diego a year ago and got my contract gig here translating for the FBI, I worked for the United Nations as a translator," I explained. "I was lucky enough to get hired there right after I earned my foreign language degrees and I loved my job there."

"I doubt it was luck," Cooper argued. "You were probably able to translate all six of their national languages."

I shook my head. "Only four. I wasn't completely competent at Chinese and Russian at the time, but I am now."

He let go of a laugh that sounded a little rusty before he said, "Okay, so you were slacking on your Chinese and Russian. Go on."

I sighed. "My last assignment was in Peru, and once I'd finished that job in Lima, I asked my boss for some time off so I could take a cruise down the Amazon and do a backpacking trip into the rainforest while I was still in the country. Because I did him plenty of favors, he agreed."

"So you obviously liked to take advantage of the travel part of your job," he commented.

I smiled back at him. "I loved seeing and exploring new places, and the Amazon Rainforest was one of those places I'd been dying to visit since I was a kid. You have no idea how excited I was to finally be there. I had a friend who hooked me up with a riverboat cruise that was leaving from Iquitos. My plan was to rendezvous with the boat in Nauta because I couldn't quite make the initial launch in Iquitos. After that, I was going to catch a weeklong hike in the rainforest. Everything went fine in the beginning. I flew from Lima to Iquitos, and then got a taxi from Iquitos to Nauta."

I knew I was rushing through the whole explanation, so I took a deep breath that forced me to slow down.

It had been a while since I'd told this entire story, and it brought back some pretty bad memories.

You can do this, Torie.

Even though a future relationship with him would never be a possibility because Cooper wasn't interested in me that way, after tonight, I really wanted to be his friend.

Maybe he didn't want a girlfriend, but I had a feeling that his choices about not wanting any new friends were more about being let down in the past than any actual lack of interest in a friendship.

I hadn't even begun to explore exactly what made this fascinating man tick, but God, I really wanted to know...

"So you got your cruise down the Amazon?" he asked. "Was it worth the rush to get there?"

I shook my head. "Before I could board my riverboat, I was kidnapped by two Amazon pirates, forced into their small boat, and taken down the river in a far different way than I had planned."

My heart sank as I saw his dumbfounded expression. "Wait," he said huskily. "Are you trying to tell me that you were kidnapped in the Amazon jungle? That you were a captive?"

I nodded slowly. "Yes. That's exactly what I'm telling you."

Chapter 5

Cooper

"Why in the fuck didn't you tell me that you were worried about Torie being alone and vulnerable in that park because it's only been a year since she was kidnapped and nearly killed?" I asked Chase irritably as I pulled a bottle of beer from my fridge. "Hell, you didn't even tell me that she *was* kidnapped. Or that she worked for the United Nations. Or that she went through one of the worst experiences a person could be forced to suffer."

"I haven't even had my first cup of coffee yet, Coop. Christ! Give me a minute," Chase answered, his voice sounding like he was only half awake. "Her kidnapping wasn't the only reason I was concerned, although I was worried she might be scared, and she just wasn't telling me that."

Okay, so it was still early morning in Paris, but I'd wanted answers the second I'd gotten home from Torie's condo. He was damn lucky I hadn't called him right that second. I'd gone out for a run and then cleaned up before I picked up my phone because it would have been really early in Paris if I'd called when I'd gotten home from Torie's place.

I hadn't asked Torie nearly as many questions as I would have liked.

It was obvious that she'd told very few people about her experience, and I hadn't wanted her to relive all of those painful memories all over again.

I could hear what sounded like Chase rummaging through the kitchen cupboard to get a mug before he said, "I'm surprised that she told you anything about it. She doesn't readily talk about it, even to me and Wyatt. And if she did tell you, why didn't you ask *her* your questions instead of waking me up so damn early?"

"She did tell me, and I'm sure she would have answered my questions, but she didn't seem all that comfortable talking about it. I thought it might be better to get the details from you," I replied, my jaw twitching with tension. "I had no idea that she joined Last Hope because she knew what it was like to actually be a hostage."

"Fuck! It's exactly something that Torie would do. One thing about her kidnapping that I can't forget is that we had no idea she was even missing," Chase shared, his voice full of remorse. "The bastards grabbed her before the riverboat staff knew she'd made it to Nauta in time to join the tour. Everyone there just assumed she'd missed the boat, and Wyatt and I thought she'd made it there on time. We didn't miss her because we had no idea that she *wasn't* on her tour. I think Wyatt and I got too accustomed to those periods when Torie was exploring out of cell phone range when she was hiking around the globe. She always told us where she'd be when she was traveling or hiking. So we didn't really worry unless she didn't call us when she was supposed to call. We always had a date and time that she was due back."

"It wasn't your fault, Chase," I assured him because he couldn't hide the anguish in his voice.

"Yeah," he answered curtly. "Try believing that when you see your little sister broken and barely alive after she's been kidnapped, starved, and beaten to within an inch of her life."

Hell, I did have a little sister, and there was nothing more I could say to him. I'd feel the same way had that happened to Riley.

I chugged down half my beer before I replied. "She said they ended up leaving her for dead in the rainforest once they found out she was a high-profile American, and that she worked for the United Nations."

"Torie played it damn smart," Chase said gutturally. "She waited until she knew what their intentions were before she said anything. And once she spoke, she pretended like she could only speak broken Spanish. So they never guarded their words when they were speaking. They were idiots and inexperienced, so they easily bought that she wasn't fluent in Spanish. She was an American. Their initial plan was to highjack the riverboat once it left Nauta, but they figured taking a lone female and asking for ransom was easier. In the end, they never implemented either plan because they decided keeping Torie and asking for ransom would probably get them captured. They beat her throughout the entire ordeal, but before they left her, they made sure she'd die in that jungle. Or so they thought. She didn't die, and she managed to crawl her way back to the river. If she hadn't been seen and rescued by some indigenous fisherman on the bank of the river, she would have died. She was damn close when they found her. I have no idea where she found the strength to get to that riverbank. These assholes may not have been experienced pirates, but they were sick fuckers, Coop. They obviously got a lot of pleasure out of hurting Torie."

"Tell me the bastards are dead or in prison," I requested hoarsely, my entire body tense.

"They were apprehended pretty quickly because of the info Torie caught when they didn't know she was listening. Neither one of them will ever see the light of day again, which is the only thing that kept Wyatt and I from finding them and killing them ourselves," Chase answered grimly. "We went to get her and bring her back to the States as soon as we were notified. She was in really bad shape, Coop. She had to spend some time in Lima being stabilized before we could even bring her home."

"I heard a list of her injuries and broken bones when the doctor was taking her medical history at the hospital. Jesus, Chase! I'm not sure how in the hell she survived that many injuries and fractures."

"She's tough. I think sheer stubbornness kept her alive because she didn't want those assholes to win. Her physical injuries healed, but Torie hasn't been the same since it happened. I'm not sure exactly how to explain it, but she lost that spark of joy she always carried along with her. She was a free-spirit, and being able to travel and hike various locations around the world meant everything to her. Her new condo in San Diego might have great views of the harbor from a distance, but I guess you have to know Torie. She's more the type to want to reach out and touch that water sometimes. It was actually kind of a big deal that she was even at the park yesterday. As far as I know, it was the first time she's ventured out to start hiking again. I hate that she hurt her ankle, but I'm relieved that she's getting outside and into something she loves again."

"It sounds like she was a pro," I told him.

"She was," he admitted. "There's not many hiking challenges she hasn't taken on over the years."

"It hasn't been that long, Chase. I'm sure she just needs some… time. I know she was a physical mess after all this happened. Was she…?" I hesitated. Hell, I wasn't even sure how to ask Chase this question. Maybe I shouldn't have even mentioned it.

"Was she raped? It's one of the first questions we ask our female captives, right?" Chase asked. "She swears she wasn't. Torie said she managed to tell them in faked broken Spanish that she had a sexually transmitted disease that would make their balls shrivel up and fall off if they touched her."

"Fuck!" I cursed. I might have laughed my ass off if I wasn't so pissed off about what Torie had been through.

"I don't think her trauma was any lighter because they didn't sexually assault her," Chase mused. "They were so damn twisted that I'm still surprised she isn't bitter toward every man on the planet. Maybe all this was why I was hoping you and Torie could be friends. She could use a hiking buddy to try to get her out more.

Her best friend is out of the country most of the time, and the rest of her friends in California have scattered over the years. She grew up in San Diego just like we did, but she didn't live there after high school. She went away to college, and then Torie worked out of New York when she was translating for the United Nations. She left her friends in New York behind, so it hasn't been easy for her to readjust to living here in San Diego again after what happened."

"I would have never known she'd been through any of this if she hadn't told me," I muttered as I raked a frustrated hand through my hair. "She seems pretty extraordinary just the way she is now."

"She is, but her true personality was a little bit different. More outgoing. More fearless, " Chase said. "Hell, she used to scare the shit out of me and Wyatt at times because she was always so damn gutsy. Her tenacity was probably the only thing that got her through that whole kidnapping ordeal. She was able to withstand two weeks as a badly abused hostage, and then she took a final brutal beating that probably should have killed her, but it didn't. After that, she crawled back to the river knowing that was likely the only way anyone would find her. Christ! She laid there for thirty-six hours on that riverbank getting eaten up by bugs until she was finally rescued. I'm not sure how many people could have survived that experience, much less bounced back the way Torie has. She might not be back to the old Torie, but her recovery is pretty damn miraculous. I get why she wants to help out at Last Hope. I think she really wants to assist other victims because she knows what it feels like to be that damn helpless. That's just the kind of person my sister is, Cooper. She has a lot more of my mom's kindness in her than Wyatt and I do."

I knew Chase's mother had passed away years ago, but he and Wyatt had obviously adored her.

Their father had died about four years ago, leaving his two sons to take over the Durand Industries empire. I'd lost track of how many luxury brands were under that umbrella, but the scope of their wealth was massive.

Because their father had been a Frenchman before he'd married an American citizen, they had a second headquarters in France, and some of their businesses were based in the City Of Light. So, there were times, like now, when they were out of the United States for a while to take care of business in Paris.

"Torie never really wanted to be part of Durand Industries?" I asked.

"Oh, hell no," Chase replied with a hint of amusement in his voice. "She swears that even though she's gifted in languages, business isn't her thing. She's actually full of shit. She manages her own very significant wealth just fine. It's not that she wasn't capable. The interest just wasn't there for her."

Sounds familiar.

My younger sister, Riley, was an environmental attorney who fought for endangered wildlife. Her passion had always been far away from Montgomery Mining, so my brothers and I had always encouraged her to chase her own dreams.

Obviously, Chase, Wyatt, and Torie's father had done the same.

"Her interests didn't really have to be in the family business," I told him. "She's incredibly intelligent and gifted in other areas."

I couldn't seem to stop cursing myself for the way I'd treated Torie simply because I'd been instantly attracted to her.

If I'd only known what she'd been through…

From the moment Torie had explained what had happened to her in Peru, I'd felt like the world's biggest asshole.

I was pretty sure I'd hurt her feelings because she'd known I'd been avoiding her every time I saw her.

Meanwhile, she was still emotionally recovering from one of the most hellish experiences a person could endure.

Godammit! I wasn't that asshole who thought I was so important that I didn't need to recognize someone else's struggles or their pain. I'd just been blinded to hers because I'd been so busy trying to protect myself.

I'd just been too caught up in my own agony of attraction to even contemplate the possibility that being a prick who avoided her might make her feel bad.

Hell, I had no idea she'd even noticed me enough to give a shit. Most women didn't.

"Once her ankle is healed up, I'll see if I can get Torie on some trails with me," I promised Chase, suddenly realizing how much I'd like to see that happen.

Maybe I was handling this whole "attraction" situation wrong in the first place. If Torie and I became friends, I'd most likely get over the desire to get her naked, right?

If Torie Durand was going to make her way back onto the trails, someone needed to be there to watch out for her as she got her bearings again.

I hiked.

I liked being outdoors as much as possible.

I was the perfect person to help her out…as a friend.

My previous reasons for not spending time in Torie's company suddenly felt extremely petty and incredibly selfish.

Truth was, I wasn't *just* attracted to her. I liked her, and I saw no reason why I couldn't get my dick under control and be her friend when she needed one.

Not that I blamed her for being wary and standoffish right now, but there was no reason for her to fight through the rest of her recovery alone. Not when I was around.

"You might find out that you enjoy her company," Chase said casually—actually, maybe a little *too casually*.

"Please tell me you aren't trying to be some kind of damn matchmaker," I said with a groan.

Just because I'd changed my mind about how to handle my attraction to Torie, that didn't mean I had any desire to…date her.

Not…really.

Fuck! What in the hell was wrong with me?

Remember Fiona?

Remember the humiliation.

Remember all of those other disastrous relationships?

Remember all of those other women who never noticed anything except your money and your name.

Do you really think a woman like Torie Durand would even be interested?

Torie doesn't need my money, and what in the hell would a vivacious, talented woman like her want with a guy who has zero imagination?

"Okay," Chase considered. "Maybe I *am* a well-meaning matchmaker. Jesus, Cooper, maybe I'm just a little tired of watching a decent guy like you torturing yourself! I don't think you've had a date since Fiona. There are very few men I'd trust to make my little sister happy, so consider my actions one hell of a compliment."

"Haven't been out with anyone," I said curtly. "It's better that way. I'm perfectly happy."

"Bullshit," he drawled. "You're just afraid to go out with another woman after Fiona. Not that I blame you. The woman was terrifying in her ambitions. I only met her a few times, but she definitely had a one-track mind that mainly revolved around social climbing."

Shit! Why was it that Chase had seen that about Fiona and I hadn't?

I'd been with Fiona for over a year. In my mind, everything had been fine, and I thought I'd finally found the one female who could tolerate my dry personality and lack of imagination.

I bought her whatever she wanted, always took her wherever she wanted to go on our date nights, and gave to her in every way I possibly could, hoping to make up for my lack of romantic words and actions.

In the end, it hadn't been enough.

It never had been enough for any woman I'd dated.

Fiona had found another guy who'd wooed her and asked her to marry him.

"I don't want a romantic relationship," I told him irritably.

"I don't buy that," Chase said stubbornly. "I think Fiona burned your ass, and now you're convinced that you can't make any woman happy."

"I can't," I answered, annoyed. "There's no damn romance in my soul."

"Did it ever occur to you that maybe you've just never been inspired?" Chase asked. "That maybe it's not you, it's the women you're dating? You have one of the highest IQs in the entire world, Coop. You're one of the most intelligent people on the planet. Hell, most of us normal folks can't even begin to understand how your mind works. Most of the women you've dated couldn't give a shit less what you're thinking about. Maybe if you found one who did, things would work out a lot better."

"Doubtful," I said testily.

"Fine," he answered with an exasperated tone. "Be Torie's friend, but don't lead her on. I don't think you realize how big of a deal it is that she actually told you about her kidnapping. She obviously trusts you. Torie might be well-traveled, intellectually gifted, and incredibly wealthy, but she's not that sophisticated when it comes to dating. She's never been one of those rich women who are clinging to a new guy every month. Even though she's a rich Durand, she's always lived a purposeful, quiet life. So if you play with her heart, I'll definitely have to hurt you."

Maybe that's one more thing that Torie and I have in common. I'm not all that sophisticated when it comes to dating, either, even though I hate to admit it. In many ways, women are still a damn mystery to me.

"Like your sister would ever be interested in me? I've never played with any woman's heart," I informed him irritably. "I wouldn't have any idea how to accomplish that, nor the inclination. Women find me incredibly boring, and much too serious. I doubt I'm Torie's dream man. She actually has a sense of humor."

"So do you," Chase argued. "It's just a lot more dry and subtle than most people can appreciate. I'm not trying to tell you what to do, but Fiona was never worth you giving up on relationships altogether, Coop."

"It wasn't just her. She was just one of the latest catalysts," I said defensively. "And you should talk. When was the last time you had a girlfriend?"

The bastard was a couple of years older than I was, and it wasn't like he was happily married and had the kind of life that allowed for criticism.

Chase dated, but he rarely went out with the same woman for very long.

"At least I haven't totally given up. I still date," he protested.

"I'm not cut out for that kind of relationship, Chase," I confessed. "I can't imagine ever losing my mind over a female like Hudson and Jax have. I'm too damn practical to let my emotions swing that wildly. I suppose that's what makes me a pretty boring romantic prospect.

"No, man," Chase denied. "That's not true. I think once you find a woman who deserves it, you'll give her fucking everything. That's the kind of guy you are, Coop, whether you see that or not."

Yeah, well, I sure as hell *didn't* see that, but Chase could be a stubborn asshole, so I didn't bother trying to argue with him. "We'll see," I muttered noncommittally before I finally ended our call.

Chapter 6

Torie

"Wait a minute," my best friend, Savannah, said the next morning as we chatted on the phone. "Are you saying that Cooper Montgomery actually carried you on his back for two miles, took care of you after he saved you, and then bought you junk food for dinner. Holy shit, Torie. If you don't want him, I think he might be my soul mate."

I snorted. "You aren't looking for your soul mate. You're way too in love with your career. I saw the piece you did on *Deadline America* a couple of nights ago. The one about the humanitarian crisis in Haiti. It was amazing, Vanna. When will you be back in the States?"

My best friend was a foreign correspondent and did the large majority of her stunning stories on one of the most popular news programs in the country.

Savannah was born to be a reporter.

I just wished that didn't mean she was out of the country so damn often in a plethora of dangerous locations.

She sighed. "I'm headed to another story in another part of the world. It could be awhile. I'll have to live vicariously through your exciting dating life now that you're dating again. My love life sucks because I'm always on the road."

"Right," I said with a laugh. "You already know there's zero action going on here. And I'm not dating Cooper Montgomery. I'm not dating anyone."

Savannah was the only one who knew everything about my kidnapping.

Sometimes I was pretty sure she just wanted to pretend like I'd have a normal dating life again someday.

Maybe I would, but I didn't see that happening anytime soon.

"Cooper Montgomery sounds interesting," she said lightly. "Obviously you've gotten close enough to him to tell him about the kidnapping."

"That's all he knows," I informed her as I rolled my eyes. "Not every guy I meet is a potential mate, Vanna," I told her. "Cooper isn't interested in a relationship with me. He was just being…nice. Yeah, I'm comfortable hanging out with him—"

"Oh, holy hell, you do like him," she said excitedly. "I know that voice, Torie. We've known each other since grade school. You're trying to pretend like you're not interested in him, but you really are. Why?"

"You know why. Besides, I told you he's not interested," I reminded her. "I'm not going to even pretend like he's not attractive, but—"

"Oh, my God," Savannah interrupted. "I just pulled up his picture on the computer? He's in a tuxedo at some event with his two brothers. He's the blond, right?"

I let go of a small sigh. All three of the Montgomery brothers were incredibly handsome, but Cooper with his golden boy looks and incredible eyes… "That's him. He's pretty hot."

"He's ridiculously gorgeous," she corrected. "And bonus….you'd definitely never have to worry about him only being interested in your money. He'd definitely be the first guy you ever dated who's richer than you are. Although I'm not sure you need a playboy billionaire in your life. Any single guy who looks like that and has that much money has to be a player."

"I don't think he is," I shared. "Honestly, I'm not sure he dates that much at all."

I could hardly tell Savannah that I knew where Cooper spent many of his evenings since I could never spill the beans about Last Hope to anyone outside of the organization. But I was aware that he hung out there a lot, and when he wasn't at Last Hope headquarters, he obviously spent some of his free time at the canine training center. Which gave him very little time to seduce a different female every night.

I heard her close her laptop. "Now that would be a shame if you're right," Savannah said. "I think you need to get him interested in dating, but only if *you're* his date."

I laughed. "Men like Cooper don't date women like me. They date supermodels or A-list celebrities. And you know I'm not into dating anyone right now."

"I know," she said wistfully. "Maybe I was hopeful that you might be if you were comfortable with Cooper. I get it. I'd shun men if I were you, too, but you might want to get back out there, eventually. I know you'd like to have a kid or two and a family of your own someday. I don't want you to lose those hopes and dreams because of what happened."

I did want a family of my own. I'd had good examples as parents and such a happy childhood myself.

I took a deep breath. "I haven't lost anything. Not really. It's not like my biological clock is ticking that loudly quite yet. I'm barely thirty-two. And finding a husband isn't the only way I can have a child. I just think if I'm meant to find the right guy someday, it could happen without me needing to kiss a bunch more frogs first."

"I still think Cooper Montgomery would be worth a smooch," she joked. "There's bound to be a prince underneath that gorgeous exterior."

"You're a hopeless romantic," I accused. "You always thought the next frog I kissed would be the one."

"I'm not really a hopeless romantic," she denied. "Maybe I'm just hopeful because you told Cooper Montgomery something that you rarely share. You never tell anyone what happened to you in the Amazon, Torie. Why Cooper Montgomery?"

I couldn't really explain why I'd been able to tell Cooper about the kidnapping.

Maybe because he was previous special forces and a member of Last Hope. So kidnapping wasn't exactly a rarity for him, right?

No, that wasn't it.

I guess it had been instinct, a feeling that Cooper wouldn't…judge.

"He's a pretty easy guy to talk to," I confessed to Savannah. "Maybe because we both know what it's like to grow up a little…different. Cooper's intellectually gifted, like me, but his intelligence is on steroids next to mine. My brothers always said that his reasoning abilities were scary, but I don't think Cooper is frightening at all. He reminds me a little of…me."

"That's great," she answered. "So you're two brilliant people who understand each other perfectly?"

I laughed. "I didn't say that."

"You've always felt like you were different, Torie," she said gently. "You're not. You've just never met a guy who appreciates all the amazing qualities you have."

"Like my creepy eyes?" I joked.

My eyes were true amber, which was a rare trait, but not one that men appeared to find attractive. Since the color could glow in the dark like cat's eyes sometimes, people considered my eyes to be more eerie than alluring.

"Your eyes are absolutely gorgeous and unique," Savannah scolded.

"Stop," I said with a groan. "I haven't found a single guy who thinks my eyes are sexy. I love you for saying that they're gorgeous, but you're full of it."

"Some guy will," she said confidently. "Wait and see. God, I wish I was there right now, Torie. It has to suck for you to be grounded and on the couch for a while after everything you've already been through."

After my recovery from all of my injuries in the Amazon, I had a really hard time being still. I'd spent so much time being immobile that it had made me half crazy to be idle anymore. "At least it won't last very long this time," I told her.

"You're essentially self-employed with the FBI since you decided not to take a full-time gig with them as a language specialist," she added.

"They can do without me for a week or so," I agreed.

I'd started doing work for the FBI to keep myself from going crazy right after I'd gotten back on my feet again.

I'd desperately needed something worthwhile and interesting to do while I was still recovering.

Working as a contract linguist for the FBI had worked out perfectly for me.

I'd felt like I was doing something that made a difference, and the FBI had gotten a skilled translator.

Win-win.

"I think they're probably still dying to recruit you full time," Savannah mused.

I smiled. "You can't recruit someone who doesn't want to be recruited. I like what I do there, but it's not my future. I'm still considering the position I was offered at the university."

"Don't rush anything, Torie," Savannah advised. "It's not like you need the money. You've just barely gotten healthy again. Well, except for the ankle thing now. Like I said, I wish I was there with you."

"You were here when I needed you," I reminded her softly.

Savannah had come home when I'd first returned from the Amazon, and having her there to talk to when I hadn't been able to speak to anyone else had saved me.

She'd stayed with me.

She'd been the friend I'd needed to lean on and talk to when I was first recovering.

She'd been the only person I could tell certain things about my captivity.

"I'm okay now, Vanna. I swear I am. I have a ridiculous ankle injury and a hesitance to travel again, which I think I'll eventually get over. I'm strong and I'm healthy. Before I turned my ankle yesterday, I was feeling like myself again. I don't think there's any way I can ever repay you for what you've done over the last year or so."

She blew off my comment. "Don't be silly," she answered. "It was just a month or two, Torie, and you would have done the same for me. I don't believe that you're totally okay, but I think you're improving every day."

I would have done the same for her, but Savannah had a much busier career to worry about than I did right now.

"I'll figure out a way to repay you someday," I warned her.

"Find me a hot date the next time I'm home in San Diego," she teased.

"I'll work on that," I said. "Right after I find one for myself. Maybe he'll have a hot brother."

"I'm pretty sure that Cooper Montgomery's brothers are already taken," she teased.

I refused to take the bait from her. She knew damn well I wasn't about to start dating again right now, much less start a relationship with Cooper Montgomery.

"Chase and Wyatt are still single," I offered eagerly.

"Oh, no," she said in a pseudo alarmed tone. "Isn't it supposed to be taboo to go after your best friend's brother or something?"

"Not really," I said cheerfully. "I'd quite happily give you either one of mine. No issues here."

"I'll pass," she said lightly. "I don't think Chase and Wyatt think of me as anything other than their little sister's pain in the ass best friend. I have to go, Torie. I have a meeting, but I'll check up on you a little later, okay?"

"Please don't worry, Vanna," I insisted. "I only called you to tell you I did something stupid. I'll be fine. Call me when you can."

"Stay off that ankle until it's healed," she demanded. "I know it's hard to keep hanging out at home, but at least you have a great view in that gorgeous new condo of yours."

My high-rise condo had a breathtaking view of the harbor, but she was right. I *was* starting to get stir crazy.

Just when I'd been ready to venture out again, I'd done something ridiculous that guaranteed I'd be staying home for a while longer.

"I'm fine. Please be careful, Vanna. I worry about you. You don't exactly find the safest places to do your stories."

"I have security," she assured me. "Don't worry. Love you. Talk soon."

I told her I loved her, too, and we'd no sooner ended our call when my doorbell rang.

"Be there in a minute," I called as I carefully stood up.

With my sore ankle, it could take a while for me to hobble across the room.

"It's just me, Torie. Take your time," Cooper Montgomery said in a sexy, low baritone from the other side of the door.

My heart did a cartwheel inside my chest.

He's here. He did show up.

Yeah, he'd promised to check on me today, but he was a pretty busy guy.

I let out a little sigh as I slowly limped toward the door.

It was totally unfair that someone as gorgeous as Cooper was so damn nice, too.

Chapter 7

Cooper

I scooped Torie up the second she opened the door, and then closed and locked the door behind me. "I probably should have asked for a key so you didn't need to get up to answer the door," I muttered as I carried her back to the couch. "How's the ankle?"

"It's okay," she said in a breathless voice. "Do you always run around sweeping women off their feet?"

"Only the ones with gimpy ankles," I told her as I set her gently on the couch.

When Torie smiled at me, I suddenly felt like I'd taken a massive punch to my gut.

Fuck!

Why did she have to be so damn beautiful?

Why did those amber eyes have to be so damn captivating?

Why did she have to…smell so damn good?

I hesitated once I'd settled her on the couch, momentarily stunned by her scent.

Her arm was still around my neck, and I couldn't stop myself from closing my eyes and taking another deep breath. "You smell good. Like a rose and some kind of sweet citrus," I told her before I could stop myself.

"It's just my body wash," she answered nonchalantly, like she didn't walk around all the time smelling like hot sex and wicked sin.

Shit! What in the fuck is wrong with me?

She was wearing a pair of black yoga pants that ended at the top of her calf. I ran my hand down her leg and gently over her injured ankle. "The swelling is down."

She shuddered a little as she nodded, her expression appearing slightly uncomfortable as she said, "It's better."

I frowned. "Are you okay?"

"Fine," she said, her voice slightly squeaky.

"It's not that much better," I replied as I rose and headed for her kitchen to get an icepack. "It's still swollen."

I couldn't shake the sense that something was wrong with Torie, but she obviously wasn't going to share.

"I took ibuprofen as soon as I got up," she called after me. "I just haven't gotten any ice yet."

"I got it," I told her as I started to fill a pack with ice.

Hell, maybe I was a masochist, but it felt right to be here with her.

I'd been edgy from the moment I'd gotten out of bed this morning, like I'd left something really important undone.

I'd taken a morning run because it had been way too early to show up at Torie's door, but that workout obviously hadn't blown off all that much steam because I was still pretty damn edgy.

I closed the icepack so it wouldn't leak as I shook my head.

Maybe I just hadn't been ready to be this damn close to temptation.

Yesterday, Torie had been riding on my back.

Today, we'd been face-to-face, with her arms around my neck.

She'd felt so good, smelled so good, that I'd had a hell of a time letting her go.

This is ridiculous. I'm not here to maul the woman. I'm here to help her out.

Like a damn friend.

Pull your shit together, Montgomery.

"How did you sleep?" I asked her as I walked back into the living room and placed the icepack on her ankle.

She hissed. "God, that's cold. You're brutal. I haven't even finished my coffee yet," she joked.

"I'm sorry," I said remorsefully. "I guess it could have waited a few minutes."

"I'm kidding, Cooper," she said with one of her killer smiles. "I want to get the swelling down. I don't want to be laid up in this house any longer than I have to be."

"Do you want more coffee?" I asked. "If you don't mind, I'll grab one for myself, too."

She shook her head and held up a half full mug. "I'm good. Please, help yourself."

I brewed a large mug for myself and took a seat in the recliner when I was finished.

"I didn't mean to just blurt out the information about my kidnapping last night," she said in a remorseful tone. "After you left, I realized it was kind of personal, and maybe something you didn't really want or need to know. You left without asking very many questions, and the last thing I wanted was to make you uncomfortable. If I did, I'm really sorry."

I shook my head. "I thought it made *you* uncomfortable to talk about it."

"Maybe it did," she admitted. "A little. There are only a few people who know."

"I talked to Chase. I told him I knew and he filled me in on some of the details." I wasn't going to lie to her. "I didn't want you to have to fill me in if it brought back bad memories. I'm sorry, Torie. I'm so damn sorry that happened to you. It's a miracle you're even alive."

She nodded and took a sip of her coffee before she said, "I feel pretty lucky most of the time. They had a gun, so they could have very easily put a bullet in my head. I was really fortunate to be found by the indigenous people in the region. What were my chances of rescue in such a remote area?" She swallowed hard before she continued. "It's been hard for me to get back to my normal life since the kidnapping. I thought if I could just get back out hiking, even if it was an easy hike, it might help. So much for that idea, right?"

Dammit! I could tell she was uncomfortable, and I hated that.

"Give yourself some time, Torie. It hasn't been that long since you totally recovered from all your physical injuries," I told her solemnly.

There was a hesitance in her expression that nearly killed me because I knew it was foreign for her to be so damn uncertain.

Of course, she was extremely wary now. It was a survivor's instinct. But that didn't mean that I wasn't sorry that those bastards had taken her ability to trust.

"I know," she confirmed. "The whole thing still just seems so surreal, Cooper. There was very little danger involved with that trip. It was something that never should have happened. I was just in the wrong place at the wrong time."

Pirate attacks happened in the Amazon, but it definitely wasn't an everyday occurrence for pirates to take an American hostage. Pirates who attacked riverboat cruises or something similar were generally just after money and expensive personal items. She was right. Plenty of foreigners took those riverboat cruises down the Amazon every day without incident. She *had* been in the wrong place at the wrong time.

"Sometimes, that just makes everything harder to understand," I replied. "If you know the risk is there, it isn't as hard to accept when it actually happens. What happened to you was highly unusual. I doubt it had even entered your mind that anything like that could happen."

"Exactly," she agreed. "When it comes out of nowhere, it takes a while to even register what's happening. After I was snatched from the dock, it took a while for what was happening to make any sense."

"Is it because of your own kidnapping that you wanted to volunteer at Last Hope? Because you've been through a hostage experience yourself?" I asked.

I had to give her credit. Most people just wanted to forget what it felt like to be held captive as a hostage. The experience was so traumatic and uncommon that they just wanted to wipe it from their brain.

"Yes. I wanted to do anything that might help other victims," she confirmed. "I heard rumors about Last Hope when I was working at the FBI offices, but I wasn't completely sure the organization really existed at first. So I started digging hard for more information. Actually, I think you guys are infamous in more than one government office. It took me a while to get a contact, but I finally got Marshall's name and number. Imagine my surprise when I found out my own brothers had been members of the group for several years and had never mentioned it to me."

"Did you tell Marshall when you volunteered?"

She nodded. "I wanted him to know the truth about exactly why I wanted to join. I didn't go into details, but I thought it was something he should know. Joining Last Hope meant something to me personally. It wasn't just a whim of some kind. Honestly, I don't want to hide my kidnapping from anyone at Last Hope, but I haven't gotten much of an opportunity to share yet. Until very recently, I wasn't even ready to talk about it."

"You don't owe anyone an explanation," I told her. "Tell people whenever you're ready or don't tell them at all if you're not comfortable. Jesus, Torie! I'm sorry for every time I acted like an idiot when we were at headquarters. I'm sorry that you thought I didn't like you, because that isn't even close to the truth. Can we start over again? Can we be friends?"

Okay. Yeah. I was attracted to her, but all I really wanted was to help her pull her life together again.

She looked together.

She acted together.

But I sensed that there was a part of her that almost no one saw, the hidden pain that hadn't really healed for her yet.

My petty bullshit just wasn't important right now.

I wasn't sure if she even wanted my friendship anymore, but if she refused, so be it.

I was tossing the idea out there just in case she still wanted to buddy up with my ornery ass.

She smiled, and that simple action lit up the entire room.

"I think once I told you about the kidnapping, I already considered you a friend, Cooper," she told me in a fond voice. "I'm really glad things will be less tense at the headquarters."

The headquarters? Wait. No.

Did she think I was just trying to make our life easier at Last Hope? "Not just there. I'd like to hang out, Torie. When your ankle is healed, I'd like to do some trails together if you're willing. Maybe you just need a partner before you start doing solo trips again. Sometimes it helps to buddy hike."

She looked slightly nervous as she answered, "I'm not really in shape to tackle anything challenging anymore. That's why I just went to the local park's hiking trails. They're familiar, and I need to get my skills back."

I shrugged. "Then we take it slow. It's not like we need to run any races. It's hiking. It's supposed to be fun."

"How fun will that be for you?" she asked. "You're so ridiculously fit that you could take on the toughest trails in the world."

"Did it ever occur to you that maybe I'd be happy just to be hanging out with you?" I asked her gruffly.

Shit! Had I really been that big of a dick? Did she really think I didn't want to be with her unless there was something in it for me?

Her eyes widened. "Actually, no. You are the one who said you weren't looking for any kind of relationship. I guess I thought that you'd rather I just leave you alone."

Yeah, I'd definitely fucked up by mentioning that out loud to her.

"I know I said that, but it's not true. Just think about it," I advised her. "I wasn't looking for any kind of relationship until I met you. I like being with you, Torie, but if—"

"I want to be with you, too. It would help me enormously to have a hiking buddy to help keep me motivated," she blurted out in a rush. "But if you really want to be friends, I need to tell you something."

"Tell me," I urged. "There's nothing you can say to me that will change my mind. I don't care whether or not those hikes are physically challenging, Torie."

She took a deep breath before she said, "I haven't hung out with or dated a guy since my kidnapping. Until yesterday, just the thought of…being touched by a male other than brothers turned my stomach."

I frowned. "Because of what happened? Hell, I can't say I blame you for that, Torie. I should have thought—"

"They raped me," she said breathlessly. "I was sexually assaulted on a daily basis, and it was inhuman and vicious."

I gaped at her, stunned by her revelation. "I thought Chase said—"

"My brothers don't know," she interrupted. "And if you really want to be my friend, you can't tell them. It's not something a sister has an easy time telling her brothers. Both of them felt guilty enough that I was kidnapped, which is absolutely ridiculous, but no one can change the way someone else feels. All I could do was try to lighten the load. There was never any reason for them to know. They were carrying a heavy enough burden and my recovery wasn't easy for them. I was completely helpless in the beginning and my brothers had to do everything for me. They don't deserve to carry another single burden over this kidnapping. It had nothing to do with them."

"You have a hard time letting a guy touch you," I said, the lightbulb finally switching on in my brain. "Just a few minutes ago when I touched your leg, you flinched a little."

"It was more surprise than fear," she explained. "I'm not sure why, but I'm not afraid of you, Cooper. I feel comfortable around you. It was just foreign to feel your hand on me, but it wasn't repulsive."

"*Fuck!* Why didn't you say something? It couldn't have been easy at the park."

I'd insisted she let me touch her when I'd told her to sit down. I'd given her very little choice except to ride piggyback. She should have told me to go to hell, but she hadn't. She'd taken a deep breath and conquered her fear.

"It wasn't that difficult," she argued. "I'm not sure if time has just taken some of my fear away, but it's kind of a big deal for me. I couldn't even handle having a male medical professional touch me right after the kidnapping. It triggered me every single time."

Christ! I couldn't blame her for that since those bastards had brutalized her like savages. If she never wanted another human with a dick to touch her again, would that be at all unreasonable?

Hell, I didn't think so.

"Who else knows?" I asked, my gut aching with the thought of just how much Torie had suffered.

"Just my best friend, Vanna, and now you. I can't tell my brothers right now. Maybe someday when things are better—"

I held up a hand. "No, I get it, Torie. I really do. I guess what really astounds me is your bravery and willingness to deal with most of this alone because you don't want to burden them."

It had taken my sister, Riley, decades to tell me and my brothers that my father had molested her as a child. I understood Torie's pain and hesitance to talk about her ordeal far better than she knew.

A lone tear streaked down her cheek. "I love them. They're all I have since Dad died, and they're always there for me. If I could spare them the details, I did. The court proceedings were all in Spanish, and none of us were there when my kidnappers were prosecuted. As long as they were put away and were never getting out, I think we were all relieved. I hated lying to them, but it was better than having them eaten up with guilt and sadness."

I raked a hand through my hair, not sure what to say to a woman like her.

The bastards that tortured her should have suffered more after everything they'd put Torie through.

"You can talk to me, Torie," I said hoarsely. "I may not know the words to say or know what to do to make your burden lighter, but whenever you need to talk, I'm here."

"It doesn't matter if you don't have the words," she said tearfully. "What matters is that you offered."

Hell, was that really enough, though? I didn't think so.

I walked over to the sofa, and I opened my arms to her. "Only if you're comfortable or if you think it will help."

Fuck! I wanted to comfort her. I wanted to hold her. I wanted to make everything okay for her again. I wanted to make all of her pain go away, but I doubted that was possible.

She didn't hesitate to throw herself into my arms and I let out a silent sigh of relief that she trusted me enough to let me touch her.

I wrapped my arms around her curvy body and rested my head on top of hers.

If I did nothing else right, I vowed that somehow, someway, I'd help this woman heal.

Chapter 8

Torie

COOPER: *I got here first. I'll get us a table.*

I smiled as I looked at his text.

Once Cooper and I had started the whole *friends* thing, we'd never really taken a break from it.

It had been almost a week since he'd held me until I felt sane again, and then hauled me out of my condo and to his training center so we could hang out with the dogs.

Okay, *I'd* played with the dogs that were too young to do much training yet.

Cooper had done some more serious training with the older dogs while I'd goofed off with the young puppies.

After that, he'd taken me to his waterfront home in La Jolla for a change of scenery.

He had an amazing house that was so close to the ocean that you could feel it, touch it, smell it, and listen to the sound of the waves hitting the beach.

After spending the entire afternoon at his place, I'd almost hated to go home, but I had returned to my condo.

However, I hadn't seen the last of Cooper.

Every day, I'd gotten another text giving me the food menu for that evening so I could choose what I wanted.

He'd spent every evening at my condo, arriving there with our food so I could keep my foot elevated.

Fortunately, I was now able to bear weight on the ankle, the swelling was gone, and I could actually walk again.

I hadn't expected to hear from Cooper this weekend since I was now mobile again, but he'd texted me earlier to ask me if I wanted to meet him at a fantastic Mexican restaurant for dinner.

He'd had me at the mention of great Mexican food and the opportunity to spend more time in his company.

ME: *I'm done here. I'm on my way.*

I'd just finished up all of my translation, so I got up from my desk at the FBI offices and grabbed my purse.

God, it had felt good to get back to work after being idle on my couch for nearly a week.

I waved at the only other translator still in the office on a Friday evening and glanced back down at my phone as it pinged.

COOPER: *Take your time and be careful.*

I grinned like an idiot as I made my way outside.

As of yet, Cooper had never ended a text without telling me to be careful.

He either cared about my safety or he was thoroughly convinced I was the most accident prone woman he'd ever met.

Luckily, the restaurant was right down the street from the FBI offices, so I didn't even have to take my car out of my parking spot.

COOPER: *Strawberry margarita?*

ME: *Yes, thank you! I think I've just decided you're the most amazing man I've ever met.*

COOPER: *Just because I got you a drink?*

I snorted. "No, you silly man," I whispered to myself. "Because you were sweet enough to think about ordering one for me."

I'd been around Cooper long enough to realize that he did nice, thoughtful things without really thinking about them.

He had no idea how endearing that quality was to me.
ME: *I'm pretty fond of strawberry margaritas.*

The restaurant was busy when I walked through the door, and it took me a minute to locate Cooper.

My heart beat faster and my breath quickened as I made my way to his table.

Just the thought of being with him the entire evening without being laid up on my sofa made me ecstatically happy.

I felt…free.

I felt…happy.

And for the first time in a long time, I didn't feel quite so alone.

Cooper and I had talked more over the last several evenings than I'd ever communicated with another guy in my entire life.

Maybe my eagerness to be with him had something to do with the fact that he always seemed eager to hear what I had to say.

He let me decide what details I wanted to share about my kidnapping. He never pushed. He just waited until I brought something up before he asked questions.

Cooper was insightful that way.

Sadly, he hadn't touched me again, but I felt his warmth in everything he did for me.

"I'm sure a handsome guy like you has a date for tonight," I said as I stopped right behind the booth. "But would you mind if I join you until she gets here?"

Our eyes met the moment he looked up at me, and my heart fluttered.

Heat flooded my entire body as he shot me a panty-melting grin. "It's about time you got here," he said in a sexy baritone. "And I'll stop you if you try to leave. You're not a substitute. You're exactly the woman I've been waiting to see."

I slid into the cushioned bench seat across from him as I asked, "How was your day?"

God, he looked amazing.

In a navy-blue custom suit, he looked every bit the wealthy and powerful man that he really was, and he wore that persona extremely well.

There were many facets to Cooper's personality and every one of them was attractive. This wealthy businessman was just one more.

His striking appearance tonight made me happy that I'd put on a skirt, a pair of boots, and a bright red sweater instead of my usual blue jeans.

"It was good," he said nonchalantly. "But it's a whole lot better now that you're here. Did you finish your work at the FBI?"

I nodded as I picked up the margarita the waitress had just delivered. "It was good to get back to work. I'm not good at doing next to nothing all day, and it's nice to actually be out in a restaurant with you."

He lifted a brow and skewered me with his gorgeous, assessing eyes. "Happy to see me or to see your margarita?" he joked.

"Both," I teased back. "I'm really glad you decided to give this whole *friends* thing a try."

"Me, too," he answered huskily as he handed me a menu. "I'm having the fajitas. What about you?"

"That was fast," I said with a laugh. "Did you even look at a menu?"

He grinned. "I'm pretty sure I've tried everything on it already."

"Then please lend me a little of your knowledge, my Obi-Wan of Mexican food. How are the enchiladas?"

"Definitely recommended. If you like spicy salsa, I'd try some of the salsa verde." He nodded at the chips and salsa on the table.

I grabbed a chip and scooped up some of the salsa. "You've heard enough about my travels to know that spicier is always better in my opinion." I popped the chip into my mouth and closed my eyes as I savored the spicy flavor of the salsa.

"That's one of the things about you that I find particularly fascinating," Cooper said thoughtfully. "When you traveled, it really sounds like you didn't just see the locations and take pictures. It's obvious you embraced the culture."

I swallowed and opened my eyes. "That's the best thing about traveling for me," I explained. "Immersing myself in a different place with people who don't do the same things, eat the same food, or have the same traditions as Americans. Not that I don't love being an American, but when I'm somewhere else, I want to experience life the way they do for just a little while."

"I haven't done as much traveling as you have," he explained. "Not for fun, anyway, and not to places I'd really like to visit."

I frowned at him. "Didn't you tell me you have a private jet?"

He nodded. "I do, but I mostly have it for Last Hope and Montgomery Mining when I need to travel to one of our mine locations. We rotate whose jet we use for every mission with Last Hope."

"But you don't use it for personal travel?" I asked, astounded.

"I suppose I would if I needed it."

I released an exasperated breath. "Cooper Montgomery, you're one of the richest men on the planet, you have a private jet at your disposal, and you're trying to tell me it's never occurred to you to just hop on that jet and let it take you to someplace different?"

He shrugged. "I guess it really never made sense for me to go somewhere for no reason."

Okay, so there was a point where a person could be way too rational and pragmatic.

"There is a reason," I assured him. "It's called pleasure, and I think you could definitely use a little of that. One of these days, when I get brave enough to travel again, I'm going to hijack that plane of yours."

The frostiness over those light blue eyes of his completely melted as he asked in a husky tone, "Are you planning on taking me hostage? I think I might like that. Also, I think you're already one of the bravest people I've ever known."

"You know that's not true," I said.

I'd already shared all of my lingering fears with Cooper. My anxiousness about some things that had never gone away after my kidnapping.

He reached out and took my hand and squeezed it. "Bravery isn't the absence of fear, Torie. Being brave is moving past that panic even though you're scared. You've done that. You keep doing it every single day."

His words and the supportive look in those gorgeous blue eyes warmed my entire soul. I blinked back tears as I replied, "I'd never consider stealing your jet without taking you hostage."

He grinned. "That certainly gives me something to look forward to."

I sent him a hesitant smile right before our waiter stopped to take our order.

Sadly, I knew that particular hostage-taking event would never take place.

Oh, I'd be ready to travel again someday, but not with him.

No matter how much I enjoyed my banter with Cooper, the two of us were just friends.

There was no possible way we could travel together without me wanting to be so much more than just a travel buddy.

My attraction to Cooper just kept getting stronger. Not only was I not afraid of him, but I was ready to climb his body like a tree and stay up there for as long as possible.

Not possible, Torie. Just keep being grateful for his friendship.

For now, and forever in the future, my threats to hijack both Cooper Montgomery and his private jet would have to remain a very pleasant fantasy.

Chapter 9

Torie

"Thank you for dinner," I told Cooper as we walked toward my vehicle after we'd finished eating. "It was delicious."

"Glad you enjoyed it," he replied. "What are you doing tomorrow?"

I didn't have any majorly exciting plans, which was sad since I was single and tomorrow was Saturday. "I was planning on checking out some of the information the university gave me about their open position as a language program manager," I shared.

"So you're going to give it serious consideration?" he asked. "I think if you decide to take it, you'll do an incredible job. They'd be lucky to have a director that's as skilled as you are in so many different languages and cultures."

"I have a communications degree, too, so it's kind of right up my alley," I confessed.

He grinned. "You neglected to mention that."

"I didn't want to sound like I was bragging after telling you about all of my language degrees, but if anyone can understand being an overachiever, it's probably you," I teased.

"But we're not talking about me," he reminded me. "And that's seriously impressive. No bragging needed. Do you think the position would make you happy? Not that you have to decide immediately since it wouldn't start until the fall."

"I think I'd like it," I said. "It would be more of a challenge. Doing only translation gets a little bit tedious sometimes."

"If you need any help deciding…" He left the thought hanging. "Never mind. I doubt you need me to lay out all the possible pros and cons of the position."

It was no secret to me that Cooper could weigh a gazillion different scenarios against each other and come up with the right option in record time.

I laughed. "I have no doubt you could give me the rational choice in ten-point-two seconds, but it's not strictly a business or logical decision. Although I might pick your brain when the time comes about some of the business duties involved."

"I'm at your service whenever you need me," he answered graciously.

"So tell me why you wanted to know my plans for tomorrow," I requested.

He shrugged in that somewhat bashful way of his that I'd come to adore. "I was trying to decide on a fun hiking excursion we could do together if you're up for it."

"Are you sure? You may get tired of seeing my face every day. If you're going to the training center in the morning, I'd love to come help out if I can. Now that I can move, I'm sure there's something I can do."

"I'd never get tired of seeing your face," he proclaimed as he moved closer, trapping my body between his and my vehicle. "And yeah, I'll be at the center in the morning if you want to come by before we leave to hit a trail somewhere."

"Thank you for tonight," I said nervously as I reached up to stroke my finger over his beautiful silk tie. "Thank you for all of this. For trying to be a friend. For listening to me talk about the kidnapping. For hanging out with me every night to keep me company."

I'd told him nearly everything else about my two-week ordeal. I might never share the gritty details about my sexual assaults, but otherwise, there was little he didn't know.

"I'm not doing a damn thing," he argued as he gently moved an errant lock of hair from my cheek and tucked it behind my ear. "Being with you isn't a hardship or a favor, Torie. It's good for me, too. I'm not sure I realized what a lonely, cynical bastard I was turning into. I look forward to every moment we spend together. And I will never, ever get tired of looking at your beautiful face. You have the most extraordinary eyes I've ever seen. Were your mother's eyes amber like yours?"

My heart began to race, but I cautioned myself against trying to make more out of this intimate moment than what was intended.

I nodded. "The color is rare and inherited. My brothers got my dad's eyes. I got Mom's. And I'm not sure how extraordinary you'd think they were if they started glowing in the dark. It freaked my college boyfriend out. He started screaming that I was a succubus, ran away, and never came back." I let out an embarrassed cough. "I thought he was being a little more dramatic than necessary."

The look on Cooper's face was incredulous as he said, "He was a moron. He obviously wouldn't recognize something sexy if it bit him in the ass."

I snorted. "Please don't tell me that you think my weird eyes are sexy."

"I can't *not* tell you that, because it wouldn't be the truth. Your eyes are breathtaking. It was the first thing I noticed about you," he said in a genuine tone. "I thought you were the most beautiful woman I'd ever seen."

My heart skipped a beat as our gazes locked.

"For a man who claims that he's not charming, you can be a silver-tongued devil when you want to be," I said breathlessly.

He shook his head. "I'm just telling you the truth and the way I see it."

And…I had to believe that because Cooper was probably the most matter-of-fact person I'd ever known.

In that particular moment, I suddenly realized that Cooper wasn't totally immune to the chemistry I felt between the two of us every single time we saw each other.

He was…attracted to me.

I knew it.

I could see it in his possessive, covetous gaze, and it was the hottest thing I'd ever seen.

"One kiss, Torie," he growled.

I knew what he meant.

One kiss.

One embrace.

One chance to taste each other and discover that our attraction didn't burn as strongly as we thought it did.

We weren't supposed to feel this way.

We were supposed to be friends. Just friends.

I grasped his tie and pulled him closer as I breathed, "Yes. Show me. Prove to both of us that all we really want is friendship."

Maybe this was what I needed to get my brain back on track when it came to Cooper.

If there was no spark, then the unrelenting sexual tension I always felt between the two of us would definitely fade away.

He cradled the back of my head before his mouth came down on mine.

Instantly, I wrapped my arms around his neck and savored every damn second that our bodies were fused together like they should have always been that way.

I moaned against his soft, voracious lips as we tried to devour each other whole.

Finally, I gave into the urge to spear my hands through his hair and luxuriate in having those coarse strands between my fingers.

I ran my short nails down the back of his neck, relishing the sensual movement and the way he reacted to it by kissing me even more frantically.

All I wanted to do was touch him. I wanted his naked skin beneath my fingers, and my equally naked body plastered against his.

"Torie!" Cooper growled as he finally pulled his mouth from mine so we could breathe. "Jesus Christ!"

He came back again and again, his teeth first nipping at my lower lip and then soothing it with his sensual embrace.

"Cooper," I moaned as his wicked mouth started to explore the tender skin on my neck. "God, yes."

Neither one of us could get enough, no matter how many times our mouths and bodies came together.

It was sensuous.

It was incredible.

It was raw and passionate.

And it was frustrating as hell because I wanted so much more of Cooper than I could get right now.

"Shit!" Cooper cursed as he backed off and scraped a hand through his usually perfect hair. "We can't do this. Proving we *didn't* really want this was a major fail. Go, Torie. Leave before I fuck this up even more."

I hesitated.

I wanted to tell Cooper that I was okay with our relationship changing.

Problem was, he apparently *didn't* want something more, even though we were definitely attracted to each other.

Friends, dammit! We're supposed to just be friends.

At the moment, I'd actually be totally willing to do friends with benefits if that's what it would take to get closer to him.

The torment I'd heard in his voice was the only thing that motivated me to fumble for my keys and slip into the driver's seat of my small BMW crossover.

As I started the car and backed out of the parking space, I wondered who in the hell I was kidding.

I could never do friends with benefits with Cooper Montgomery.

Because of the intensity of my emotions for Cooper, a relationship like that would chew me up and spit me out.

He was an all-or-nothing guy for me.

And because he obviously didn't feel our crazy attraction with the same intensity I did, he had to be my…nothing.

D. A. Scott

As I pulled out onto the downtown street, pent-up tears I hadn't shed for a very long time began flowing down my cheeks like a river.

I kept driving without looking back, leaving Cooper Montgomery and that damn devastating kiss behind me.

Chapter 10

Cooper

"I have no idea what I was thinking," I confessed to my two older brothers the next day—after I'd explained most of what had happened with Torie and how I'd failed a "just friends" relationship with her. "She's Chase and Wyatt's younger sister, for fuck's sake, and a member of Last Hope."

I hadn't mentioned her kidnapping since that was probably something Torie should tell people in her own time.

Friends! All she needed was a goddamn friend to help her through some of the rough patches she was experiencing, but I hadn't been able to keep my filthy hands off her. I hadn't been able to keep my mind off every lustful fantasy I had about Torie, either, dammit!

Hudson had invited Jax and I over to his place this afternoon since Taylor and Harlow had decided to have lunch and do some wedding shopping for Taylor and Hudson's wedding this spring or summer.

The three of us were hanging out on his patio near the beach, drinking a few beers.

It had been a long time since I'd had a really candid discussion with my brothers. Since I had no idea what to do about Torie, I figured maybe today might be a good day to be a little more open with them.

Jax shrugged. "It's not like you can decide who you're attracted to, Cooper."

"Maybe not," I answered, feeling restless and impatient. "But I should be able to decide on whether or not to act on that attraction."

Hudson snorted. "Good luck with that. With the right female, there's no such thing as a choice. The attraction is too damn overpowering."

"Maybe for you two," I shot back. "I don't lose my head over a woman. Never have."

"Bullshit," Jax said with a smirk. "You just told us that you lost it. You either did or you didn't."

"Fuck! Okay. I failed to keep her at arm's length," I said reluctantly.

Hudson coughed. "Sounds like you failed at trying not to shove your tongue down her throat until you found her tonsils, too."

Jax smirked. "You've never completely lost it before because you've never met the woman who could break you with a single look. Have you ever considered that maybe Torie could be that Achilles' heel?"

"No," I grumbled. "I gave up on romantic relationships over a year ago. We're just supposed to be friends. Things just got…a little out of hand."

Hell, those words sounded hollow, even to me. It wasn't like I hadn't always known I was physically attracted to Torie.

I saw her, my dick got hard, but I'd been able to control it…until last night.

I wasn't even sure what had happened.

Had I wanted to prove to her that we could keep being friends without the attraction getting in the way, or had I really needed to test it myself?

Nah! I was man enough to admit that I'd *wanted* to kiss her, goddammit!

I wasn't going to hide behind all that testing bullshit.

Fuck! Either way, it had been a complete fail. I wanted Torie in a way I'd never experienced before, and in a way that made no damn sense.

Hudson lifted a brow. "Maybe you should reconsider that friendship decision. It doesn't sound like it's working for you. Is that why you've been such an asshole? Because you haven't gotten laid in over a year?"

Okay, maybe I should have known better than to tell Hudson and Jax that it had been…a while.

"It's not like I decided to become a monk," I replied. "The opportunity just hasn't come along…recently."

Christ! Did my brothers really need to know exactly how long it had been for me?

No. No, they really did not.

If they knew too much I'd probably never hear the end of it since I'd given them a hard time about losing their minds over Harlow and Taylor.

"What happened with Fiona, Coop?" Jax asked in a calm, patient voice that he didn't use very often. "You haven't been the same since you two broke up. Maybe I'm wrong, but you never acted like you were madly in love with her."

"I don't think I was," I confessed. "But I was content."

"Contentment isn't enough for a lifetime commitment," Hudson commented.

I shot him a dirty look. "Maybe it's not for you, but maybe it was for me. Fuck! Forget I said that. You're right. It wasn't enough because she didn't give a damn about me. Just my money and the Montgomery name. That's the way my relationships always turn out. Unlike you two, I've never met a female who gave a shit about me. I've never been charming. I've never known exactly what to say to a woman to make her happy. My brain doesn't work that way. I'm just…honest. Which is apparently the same as being boring and unimaginative if you ask any of the women I've dated."

"Because you weren't dating the right women," Hudson replied. "Fiona was a social climber that probably had very few intelligent thoughts in her head. Same with the rest of the women you've dated in the past. Have you ever considered that it was their problem and not yours, Coop? That maybe they just weren't smart enough to see all of your good qualities."

Okay, so maybe hearing that theory for a second time made me pause. Hudson was saying the same thing that Chase had told me not long ago.

I folded my arms over my chest and shot Hudson a dubious look. "I've dated quite a few women. Are you trying to tell me that they were all wrong about me being uninspired?"

"That's what I'm saying," Hudson agreed with a nod. "Because they were all the same type of women. Is that an issue with Torie? Surely the two of you can have an intelligent conversation."

I shrugged. "I didn't ask her if she thinks I'm boring and uninspired. We aren't dating, but she never seems like she's bored."

"Well, maybe you two should date," Jax suggested. "She's definitely more your type."

"What makes you say that?" I asked curiously.

I'd never really had a type.

Jax took a slug of his beer before he answered. "You need a woman you can have an intelligent conversation with, and someone who has some of your same interests. Hell, Fiona didn't even like to walk outside to get from a building to her car because it messed up her hair. You can't spend your life with someone like that, Cooper. You were settling, and I have no idea why. There are plenty of women outside of our old social circle, educated women who would love to go out with a guy like you. There's nothing wrong with you. You're intelligence on steroids, but all that means is that you need a different type of female from the ones you've dated in the past. Maybe they did find you boring, but I'm sure those thoughts went both ways. You've just never admitted to yourself that those women pretty much left you completely numb."

"What do you want, Coop?" Hudson asked bluntly. "Honestly."

"Hell, I don't know," I answered, feeling frustrated. "Maybe I do want what you two have now—minus the losing my mind part of it. I guess I want a woman to see me instead of just lusting after my money and the Montgomery last name. It's just never happened for me."

As much as I might bitch about how crazy my brothers were about their women, Harlow and Taylor adored my brothers just as much.

I had to admit that there was something special about those two relationships, and that maybe part of me wanted something…similar.

"Hudson and I wanted a woman to see us, too, even before we got that. We went through our share of senseless relationships with women who only wanted our money and notoriety," Jax said in a low, serious tone. "We just never recognized exactly what we wanted until we had it right in front of us, and we still almost managed to fuck things up. Maybe because we never thought we deserved the kind of love we get from Harlow and Taylor. Or maybe we just didn't understand it at first. Fuck knows, we never saw it growing up, but don't let your past define your present or your future, Cooper. Fight for what you want and know that if you do, it will be a hell of a lot different than the twisted relationship our parents had."

"Obviously, Torie is different from all of the other women you've dated," Hudson mused.

"That's putting it mildly," I informed him. "I have no fucking idea what to do with a woman like her. She actually seems to like being with me. For no reason. She doesn't need my money or my name. Hell, the Durand name is even more prestigious than ours, but she doesn't seem like she's into that social crowd."

"So drop the whole I'm-not-looking-for-a-romantic-relationship bullshit. Jesus Christ! I'm surprised you haven't managed to scare her off with that shit yet," Hudson instructed. "Give it a real chance with her. If Torie cares, it won't be because of your money or your name. You're right. She already has those things, Cooper. She's obviously just interested in…you."

"Maybe that's the part that actually scares me," I said, thinking out loud. "What can I offer a woman like Torie who already has everything?"

Jax shrugged and shot me a grin. "It's a bitch when you meet a woman who wants nothing to do with your money or your name. There's not much to give her that would mean anything to her except your heart."

"I almost think I'd rather just give her my money and my name," I grumbled. "You guys know I'm a cynical bastard. I don't believe in love the same way you do."

"It might be safer that way," Hudson agreed. "But something really worth having means taking the risk. Believe me, if you want a relationship that means something, you have to give more than just your money."

"What happens if that woman doesn't want your heart?" I asked.

"Then she was the wrong woman," Jax said simply.

"Even if I wanted to try to fix things with Torie, I doubt she'd give me that chance after I screwed things up so spectacularly. We were supposed to be building a friendship. I should have never kissed her like that. I just kind of…lost control."

Two sets of eyes flew to my face.

I held up a hand. "Give me a break. I'm not nearly as crazy as you two."

Jax chuckled. "Give it time."

"It's not like you can completely ignore each other," Hudson said. "You're going to see each other at Last Hope."

I ran a frustrated hand through my hair. "I don't want to pretend like she's not there anymore," I admitted. "I don't think I can. I just don't know if she really needs a guy who's that damn attracted to her, either. She…got hurt and hasn't been all that into dating in the last year or so."

Hell, what else could I say?

"I wonder how you'll feel if she starts dating someone else," Jax mused.

Bastard. He was needling me, and he knew it.

Unfortunately, it was working.

Someday, she would completely heal.

Someday, she would let other men touch her.

Someday, she would start dating. She was far too amazing and beautiful not to be inundated with guys who wanted to date her.

I knew with certainty that I'd hate myself for not trying to win her over myself.

"Stop," I growled. "I've already decided to let Torie choose exactly where this goes. I texted her earlier, and she hasn't answered me. I'd say her silence speaks volumes."

"I'd say she's pissed," Hudson countered. "You don't kiss a woman like that, and then tell her to go away, Coop. Jesus! Did you really expect her to just fall right back into a friendship again after you confused the hell out of her?"

"I'm not sure what I expected," I told him. "That kiss practically rocked my entire world. I was within a hair's breadth of trying to convince her to go home with me, even when I knew that all she needs is a friend right now."

Jax chuckled. "Good luck with that struggle. I went through the same damn thing with Harlow. She'd been through hell and back, but the chemistry between us still couldn't be denied, no matter how much I wanted to ignore it. There are no rules or etiquette for some emotions, Coop. They're relentless and they're messy."

"I've done that very same struggle. You could try apologizing," Hudson suggested.

"I could. That's actually what I tried to do when I texted her, but she didn't answer," I told him. "Truthfully, I'm not sure how sorry I really am about what happened. I only regret the way I handled it. I should have been there for Torie instead of pushing her away."

Fuck! I really had no idea how to deal with a woman who actually liked me or cared about how I felt.

"Don't try to make sense out of what happened," Jax warned. "You'll never be able to do it, and your brain will explode. Emotions and reasoning don't mix very well."

"Yeah, I'm starting to understand that," I said drily.

"Time is on your side," Hudson said. "You two will see each other at Last Hope. She'll eventually talk to you if you're persistent."

I nodded. "I plan on being the steadiest guy she knows in the future."

Hudson was right.

It wasn't like I'd never see Torie again.

The problem was, I knew it was going to eat my guts out until I knew she was willing to forgive me for a knee-jerk reaction that never should have happened.

Chapter 11

Torie

I listened as the two pirates debated whether or not to put a bullet through my brain.
They were arguing in rapid-fire Spanish, but I understood every single word.

My body shook with pain and fear, knowing I could very well be living the last seconds of my life.

Maybe I should be hoping for a quick death at this point.

I could scarcely draw in enough breath to oxygenate my body because so many of my ribs were broken.

Honestly, there weren't many parts of my body that weren't burning with pain, but I still wanted to live.

Relief flooded through me as the two men decided that they didn't want to fire their weapon unless absolutely necessary because it might draw unwanted attention to their presence.

I wanted to weep with gratitude as I lay there on the forest floor, dirty and bloody from all of my previous beatings.

My captors were psychopaths who enjoyed watching other people suffer.

My happiness over my respite lasted all of two minutes, which was exactly the amount of time that passed before I realized that they were going to make sure I was dead or damn close to it before they departed. Even though they weren't going to shoot me in the head.

They'd just changed their plan from a bullet through my brain to beating me until I wasn't breathing instead.

I closed my eyes before they could see that they were open.

Maybe I could pretend like I was already dead. Lord knew I had enough injuries for that to be believable.

Unfortunately, they could tell that I wasn't dead because I couldn't control the shaking.

A few swift kicks to my head stopped the incessant tremors and had me sliding toward darkness...

I came awake from my nightmare, just like I always did.

My body bolting upright in bed, and my lungs sucking in a deep breath as I awakened.

I panted heavily as I assured myself it was just a bad dream.

It was just an awful nightmare.

It wasn't real.

Unfortunately, I had no luck convincing myself of that because I knew the real truth.

It was less of a dream and more like a recreation of actual events.

I just couldn't seem to stop experiencing the worst of my trauma in the jungle over and over again in my nightmares.

I reached for my cell phone and took a quick look at the time.

One o'clock in the morning.

My hands shook as I considered calling Savannah, but I had no idea what part of the world she was in right now.

I certainly couldn't call my brothers since I hadn't told them that I still had recurring nightmares. They'd been worried enough over the last year. I'd never seen the point in telling them about my persistent nightmares.

Tears flowed down my cheeks as I flipped to my text messages, and the two words that Cooper had sent earlier caught my eye.

COOPER: *I'm sorry.*

Earlier, those words had angered me because I wasn't the least bit sorry about what had happened.

I didn't regret the most amazing kiss I'd ever experienced in my life, but I had been destroyed that he didn't feel the same way.

I knew he'd listen if I needed to talk, and God, I was tired. So tired…

I'd been fighting the effects of sleep deprivation for so long…

Before I could stop myself, I fired off a message.

ME: *Are you still awake? I could use someone to talk to right now.*

It didn't take more than a moment or two to get a response.

COOPER: *I'm here. You okay?*

I shook my head as another tear trickled down my cheek.

ME: *No.*

My phone rang seconds later, and I answered his call immediately.

"What's wrong?" Cooper asked, his voice concerned.

"You have to make me a promise," I told him in a tremulous voice. "You can't say a word to my brothers. They don't know."

"I promise," he replied in a solemn baritone. "I'd never reveal anything you asked me not to talk about."

"Nightmares," I choked out, still disturbed by the vivid images of my dream. "For a while, the bad dreams slowed up a lot, but they started again almost nightly about a month ago. They're really short, mostly just snippets of the really bad things that happened. Kind of like flashbacks while I'm sleeping. It's never easy to get back to sleep once it happens."

"You're still upset. You just woke up from one of them," he guessed.

"Yeah. It was terrifying. The kidnappers were discussing whether or not to put a bullet in my head. Once they decided not to do it, I realized that they were going to beat me until I was dead instead. Once that started, I woke up. That's usually the way it happens. Short but terrifying. I know I'm safe once I wake up but it's really hard to go back to sleep again. I'm really tired, Cooper."

My nightmares were one of my biggest setbacks. The less sleep I got every night, the worse my anxiety became over the bad dreams. It was a vicious cycle I hadn't been able to break.

"Jesus, Torie," Cooper rasped. "Why didn't you tell me you were still having nightmares? It has to be hell reliving that shit every night."

"It's exhausting," I whispered. "I'm sorry if I woke you. I just… panicked for a moment. There's always that short period of time right after a nightmare when you want to talk to somebody, you know?"

"I'm here. Do you want me to come over?" he asked, sounding like he was ready to get in his vehicle if that's what I needed.

"No. I'll be okay. Just…talk to me for a few minutes?" I requested as I turned on my beside lamp.

"All night if you need me," he said hoarsely. "Do you want to talk more about the actual dream?"

"No," I said hastily. "I've lived it. Distract me, please."

"How about I tell you again that I'm sorry about last night," he said.

I shook my head. "Don't. Maybe you regret it, but I'm not sorry. I never knew a kiss could be like that, so I just can't wish it had never happened. Not after everything that's happened to me. It gives me hope that I can be normal again someday, Cooper. That I can completely separate what happened to me and label it as a vicious crime so I can move on and have a normal relationship with a guy in the future. That kiss gave me that hope. It gave me pleasure, Cooper. I refuse to let go of it and pretend like it didn't happen or that I didn't thoroughly enjoy it."

"I'm not sorry about the kiss, Torie. I'm sorry about the way I handled it. I flipped out when that wasn't really necessary. I sent you away instead of explaining, and I really can't blame you for being so pissed off that you didn't answer my earlier text."

"That's not why I didn't answer," I said softly. "I didn't know what to say because I wasn't sorry, and yeah, maybe I was a little pissed off because you were."

"I acted like an idiot," he grumbled.

I rolled my eyes and flopped back onto my pillow. "You're far from being an idiot, Cooper. There's a really powerful physical attraction between us. Maybe the timing sucks. Maybe it would be better if

I wasn't attracted to you and we could just be friends, but it's there and I can't completely ignore it. It's enough to confuse the hell out of anyone. Especially when all we really want in our logical mind is a friendship. But I have no idea how to stop being attracted to you."

"Me, either. Hell, I'm not even sure if I want to let go of that attraction, even if we could. There's no excuse for the way I treated you. We should have talked about it instead of me trying to push you away. The question is…where do we go from here, Torie?" he asked in a graveled voice.

"I'm not sure," I said honestly. "Neither one of us is looking for a relationship."

"But now that we know that our attraction isn't going away, a friendship only relationship is almost impossible. I admit that the timing completely sucks. All you need is a friend right now," Cooper answered. "I propose that we call our outings 'dates' from now on if you're still willing to go out with me. It could be an experiment for you, and a way to find your way back to normal again. You could consider me your…test date. When I swore off dating, I never expected to meet someone like you, Torie. We can take things slow. At least we won't have to try to hide our attraction anymore, but we don't have to do anything about it right now, either. We can just move on kind of like friends, but knowing that attraction is there. It will be up to you to decide what you want when you're ready."

So, he was basically leaving it up to me to decide what I wanted from him.

I swallowed hard. "You were totally unexpected for me, too. I'm game for casual dating if you are." I hesitated before I asked, "I guess what I don't understand is why you were so adamant about *not* dating anyone. Did someone hurt you, Cooper? I'll probably never understand why an amazing guy like you isn't already involved with someone who adores you."

"Women don't adore me, Torie. My longest relationship lasted a year," he explained. "I thought we were in an exclusive relationship. She didn't. I stopped over at her apartment one night with a bottle of wine and a pair of diamond earrings she'd been hinting about. She'd been complaining that I was never spontaneous or romantic, so I decided to try to surprise her. I knew she was right, and I wanted to make up for being a lousy boyfriend. She had another guy in her bed that night because she wasn't expecting me and I never did anything out of the ordinary. All she really wanted was to marry a rich man, and it turns out that to her, all of us were interchangeable. She ended up married to Craig Appleton a few months ago."

Craig Appleton?

Because I'd been raised in the upper class society in San Diego, I knew exactly who he was talking about, even though I didn't hang out with that crowd on a regular basis.

"Wait a minute," I said in a horrified tone. "Are you trying to tell me that some woman actually dumped you for…him?"

God, was that even possible? I'd met Craig Appleton and there was no comparison between a man like Cooper and that ridiculous man.

"Yep. That's exactly what I'm saying," he confirmed.

"Good Lord, she must have been a complete idiot. He's always been a mean little halfwit, and she can't be much better if she dropped the hottest billionaire on the planet for someone like Craig Appleton. No offense, but I think you probably dodged a bullet with that one," I grumbled. "She didn't deserve you, Cooper."

"I think you might be right about dodging a bullet," Cooper said hoarsely. "She's definitely not the woman I was supposed to end up with long-term. So, dinner tomorrow?"

I smiled. "I'll check my calendar, but I'm pretty sure I'm free."

"I'll pick you up around five," he said immediately.

"Early dinner?" I asked.

"More like an eager date," he answered, his tone self-mocking. "Are you feeling a little less anxious about your nightmare? Honestly, Torie, it wouldn't take me long to get there."

My heart squeezed at his willingness to jump into his vehicle just because I was struggling.

"No. I feel a little better," I told him. "I guess I should be used to these damn nightmares by now."

"Hell, no," Cooper growled. "No one should have to just get used to having nightmares. I know someone who does some progressive therapies for this, Torie—"

"I've been in therapy for post-traumatic stress since it happened," I shared.

"And I'm sure your therapist is good, but there might be better therapies for what you went through. This particular psychologist has been working with Last Hope rescues for years, and she's had tremendous success with flashbacks and nightmares. This is her specialty, and she's done some amazing things for some of our victims. Just a thought."

I sighed. "I'm willing to try something different. It helped to talk about it with my counselor in the beginning, but that doesn't seem to be working anymore."

"I'll arrange it," Cooper replied. "Are you going to be okay tonight, Torie?"

"I'll be fine," I assured him with a yawn. "Thank you for being here to talk to me. I'll try to get back to sleep. Go to bed, Cooper. I'll see you tomorrow."

"Call if you need me," he said in a no-nonsense tone. "I mean it."

The gesture was so sweet that I didn't call him on his bossiness.

"I will. I'm sorry someone hurt you, Cooper. You didn't deserve that, but it really was her loss. Night," I said softly.

Once we'd disconnected the call and the bedroom was silent again, I realized just how well Cooper had managed to distract me.

I shut off the bedside light and closed my eyes, most of the horrific images from earlier gone.

I fell asleep thinking less about the kidnapping and more about what it was going to be like to have a real date with Cooper Montgomery, casual or not.

Chapter 12

Cooper

"Don't bother calling in an order for food. I brought lunch," I told my brothers as I strolled into Jax's office nearly a week later.

I could tell that my siblings were searching for lunch options since both of them were going through a pile of menus that Jax kept inside a file in his desk.

Hudson tossed the file onto Jax's desk and gaped at me as I sat multiple paper bags down on the desk.

"Italian?" Jax asked as he eyed the logo on the bags. "Sounds good. Jesus, Cooper, you're way too accommodating and weirdly cheerful. Did you fall down and get some kind of head injury?"

I shot my brother a dirty look as I sorted out the food. "Nice," I said drily. "I go and get you two lunch, and that's the kind of gratitude I get?"

Hudson shook his head, and there was a smirk on his face as he added, "I have to agree with Jax. Something's up. You've been in a really good mood all week. What's up?"

I unpacked the food and gave my brothers their favorites. All three of us knew this Italian restaurant well, so I'd known exactly what to order for Hudson and Jax.

I pulled out my pasta dish and pulled the top off of it, and then grabbed a piece of bread as I answered, "Nothing is up."

Jax shook his head as he opened his container of lasagna. "I'm betting it has something to do with a woman you're now…dating."

I took a chair next to Hudson, while Jax had settled in behind his desk to eat. "What do you two know about my dating life?"

Hudson shot me a sideways glance. "You're joking, right? As the only unattached Montgomery sibling left, do you really think you can keep something like that a secret?"

Actually, I wasn't keeping it a secret. I simply hadn't had much time to fill my brothers in on what had transpired. "Torie is calling it casual dating," I informed them.

"Ouch!" Jax exclaimed. "And how are you dealing with that?"

I shrugged. "There's absolutely nothing wrong with taking things slow. She's been through a lot over the last year. I think it would be a mistake to push her too hard or ask for too much."

Torie had decided to share her kidnapping experience with everyone at Last Hope and not just Marshall, so my brothers knew all of the basics, minus the information about the sexual assault.

"Yeah, Hudson and I tried that whole taking it slow thing, too," Jax told me. "Word to the wise…it nearly killed us."

"It was absolutely impossible in my case," Hudson grumbled.

"Maybe I'm a little more patient than you two," I suggested.

"You're obviously happy, no matter what speed this relationship is moving," Hudson observed. "Are you planning on bringing her to my barbecue on Sunday? Riley and Seth are coming down from Citrus Beach."

I hadn't seen my sister Riley in a while, so I did want to go… "I'm just not sure that Torie is ready for that yet," I said thoughtfully. "You know, the meet-the-family thing."

Truthfully, I'd never done the meet-the-family thing with any woman. Probably because none of them had ever really wanted to simply hang out with my siblings.

"It's not like she won't know everyone already," Jax said. "Once Harlow noticed that you and Torie seemed to be dating when she saw you guys at Last Hope headquarters, she told Taylor. Then Taylor called Riley. The news was big enough to warrant an emergency happy hour meeting tonight. Harlow already invited Torie to go since they've gotten to be friends at Last Hope."

I groaned. "Seriously? Torie hasn't mentioned it. You know our little sister is going to grill her half to death."

"On the other hand," Jax said calmly. "Riley will also sing your praises and tell Torie what an amazing guy you are the whole time they're together."

Yeah, okay, so maybe the women meeting up wouldn't be such a bad thing.

"I just don't want her to feel uncomfortable," I said.

"You know Riley, Taylor, and Harlow better than that," Hudson said. "They'd never push things so far that Torie wasn't comfortable. They all adore you, although I have no idea why."

"I'm sure you're right," I conceded. I didn't want to piss Jax or Hudson off by inferring anything negative about Taylor and Harlow. Hell, I adored both of them, too. I just wished they hadn't decided to ambush Torie quite this soon.

"So you'll bring her with you Sunday?" Hudson asked.

I nodded. "I'll invite her and we can probably stop by. We haven't really solidified any of our plans for the weekend. Now that her ankle is healed, we were going to visit the dog training center in the morning and take an easy hike tomorrow afternoon. We didn't discuss anything about Sunday."

For a couple who were just "casual dating," Torie and I had spent a hell of a lot of time together this week.

We had dinner together every single night.

Not that I was complaining...

It was always my suggestion because I was addicted to seeing her and being with her every day.

"So is Torie the reason you're in the best mood I've seen from you in a very long time?" Jax asked.

Jesus! Had I really been that big of a dick? "Probably. I enjoy every moment that we spend together," I answered simply. "It doesn't really matter what we're doing."

"Happy for you, Coop," Hudson said sincerely. "You've been miserable for way too long. Torie is the type of woman who is really going to appreciate a brilliant guy like you, and not be intimidated by that intelligence."

"I think she definitely finds me a lot less boring than most women do," I agreed.

"You were never boring," Jax corrected. "Your dates just never had enough brains to have a conversation with you."

I shook my head. "It's not like I tried to get into philosophical or scientific discussions with them," I explained. "All I ever really wanted was to talk about something…anything except the gossip about the wealthy and socially elite crowd. I might be rich, but it's not like I have any good friends in that social group. I have no idea why everyone wants to know every damn time they take a piss."

Hudson nodded. "I think we all learned what real friendship was like once we got into the military. I can't imagine hanging out with the crowd we grew up with anymore."

"Ditto. I have no friends there either," Jax added. "So how are Chase and Wyatt going to handle the fact that you're dating their little sister?"

"Why would they care?" I asked him with a frown.

He shrugged. "I'm not saying they would care, but let's not forget the hell we put Seth through before he got our blessing. I can only imagine how protective they are after what happened to her in the Amazon."

"Chase was actually trying to play matchmaker," I told them. "I think he wants to see Torie and I dating. Although he did say that if I played with Torie's heart, he'd have to hurt me."

Hudson chuckled. "Sounds like something he'd say."

I tossed my empty container into the trash and reached for my dessert. "Torie isn't the type of woman who would let her brothers run her life. She loves them and she cares about worrying them unnecessarily, but she'd put her foot down just like Riley always did when we tried to push our advice on her a little too hard."

Jax chuckled. "Is that what we're calling it now? *Pushing our advice too hard*? I think Riley would say those were the times when we got way too arrogant and bossy."

"She was probably right," Hudson said. "In the end, she did just fine without our help. She found a career she loves and there probably isn't a better guy for her than Seth. She knew what and who was going to make her happy."

"It's not like she's never tried to meddle in our lives," I commented. "She is going for drinks with a woman I just started dating."

"With our women," Jax added with a grin. "Welcome to our world."

"But you like that, right?" I asked. "You're glad that Harlow and Taylor get along well with Riley?"

Hudson laughed. "They do a lot more than just get along. The three of them are thicker than thieves. But yeah, I like it. Riley has been a good friend to Taylor when she really needed one. I'm glad they're close."

"Same," Jax chimed in. "I'm glad the three of them are tight. I think Torie might like joining the club. She's in the same boat that Riley has always been in. Older brothers but no sisters."

I nodded. "I think she misses her friends in New York and her best friend that travels around the world as a journalist. She grew up here in San Diego, but you know how that goes…friends get married and they scatter over the years. I know it's not the same for Torie here anymore. She hasn't lived here since high school."

"Do you think she regrets giving up her job at the United Nations?" Hudson asked.

"Nah, I doubt it," I answered honestly. "She could have gotten that job back in a heartbeat once she recovered. I think she wants to do more than just translate. She hasn't made a decision yet, but she was offered a job at the university as the director of their language program. I think she might end up taking it."

"I'm not surprised," Hudson said. "She's so damn talented that any number of employers would probably fight over her."

"Honestly, she doesn't really have to do anything," Jax said thoughtfully. "Just like Riley. Both of them could have let themselves get sucked into the social scene and spend all of their time doing useless things like our mother."

"Glad they didn't," Hudson said gruffly.

I shook my head. "I can't see either one of them falling into that lifestyle. Even when they were younger. I think Riley was always driven to get out of that whole way of life. She hated it."

"And Torie was raised by normal parents," Jax added. "Chase and Wyatt are so damn solid that I couldn't see Torie being any other way."

I nodded absently as I finished off my dessert.

Torie was so different from every other woman I'd ever met or dated.

She was brilliant.

She was funny.

And her world was so much larger than most of the women I'd gone out with previously.

I took a glance at my watch as I pictured Torie's gorgeous, smiling face.

I hoped the women were planning on getting together early.

I loved my sister and Harlow and Taylor.

However, I did have what I considered an important dinner date with Torie later, and I selfishly wanted to make sure it was still going to happen as planned.

Chapter 13

Torie

"Cooper has always been different," Riley told me after she took a long sip of her cocktail. "Not different in a *bad way*. For instance, when we were young, if Hudson or Jax noticed that I was sad, they wanted instant gratification. They'd tickle me or tease me until I smiled. Cooper was more likely to take me out for ice cream and try to get me to talk about why I was sad. Do you understand what I mean?"

I nodded and took a sip of my own drink. "I could see that."

"Me, too," Harlow chimed in from her seat across from me and Riley. "That sounds like Jax."

"That's Hudson, too," Taylor said from her seat next to Harlow. "When he wants a problem solved, he wants it to happen immediately."

"Cooper is just the kind of guy who looks at things from every angle," Riley explained. "He's cautious and careful because he doesn't want to be wrong."

I turned my head and smiled at her.

I really liked Cooper's sister and Hudson's fiancée, Taylor.

I already knew Harlow from our interaction at Last Hope, and I'd liked her from our first meeting.

Turned out that Taylor and Riley were just as sweet as Harlow.

Did I *know* that Riley was checking me out because I was dating her brother?

Yeah, I knew. I had two older brothers myself, so I'd caught on immediately. But she'd been so kind that I really didn't mind.

In some ways, I totally understood her.

If one of my brothers was dating someone new, I'd probably try to find a way to meet her, too.

I wished my brothers would be as lucky in love as the two eldest Montgomery brothers had been, but I didn't see that happening anytime soon.

Wyatt was getting closer and closer to forty with zero desire to marry as far as I knew.

And Chase? He never seemed to take any relationship seriously.

One thing I didn't agree with Riley on was her statement about Cooper being *different*.

Cooper Montgomery was unique, and his intelligence seemed to make him exude a hot, broody, mysterious persona that spoke to every female hormone in my body.

Maybe he was a little complicated, but that just made him all the more fascinating.

I shot a quick glance at my watch and realized that we'd been in this bar for almost two hours.

I'd been with Riley, Harlow and Taylor long enough for me to spill my guts about my kidnapping and my subsequent return to San Diego after it happened.

I had to be careful what I said because Riley didn't know a thing about Last Hope.

Yeah, I understood that it was a secret organization, but since Hudson and Jax had been involved almost from the beginning, I was a little surprised that they'd never told their sister.

"I'll probably have to go soon," I said with no small amount of regret. "I'm supposed to meet Cooper at his place. He's arranged almost every meal for us since I hurt my ankle. I told him I was cooking for him tonight."

I'd had such a good time with these women that I was going to hate to leave our cozy booth that all of us had commandeered in a quiet back corner of the bar.

Riley made a face. "I'm glad you're cooking because Cooper is a horrible cook."

"Your mother never taught him to cook?" I asked curiously.

My brothers might not always have the time to cook and do laundry themselves, but they were perfectly capable of those tasks. My mother had been insistent that none of her children would become quite that privileged and helpless.

The entire table went silent.

Finally, Riley spoke, "Our family was really dysfunctional, Torie. Maybe Cooper hasn't told you much about it, but not a single one of us speaks to my mother. Our father died years ago."

I listened, horrified as Riley revealed that she'd been molested by her father, but her brothers hadn't found out until after her parent was already dead.

"My mother was no better," Riley explained. "She covered everything up, which is why none of us want to have anything to do with her. Not to mention the fact that neither one of our parents were exactly loving. My father was terrifying and we could never do anything right as far as he and our mother were concerned."

I swiped a tear from my cheek as I said, "I'm so sorry, Riley. That must have been horrible. I guess I can't imagine any parent acting that way. My mom died of cancer when I was a teenager, but I always knew I was loved by her and by my father, who died four years ago."

I didn't know what it was like not to have loving support from my parents and from my older brothers.

Riley shook her head. "I got over what he did to me a long time ago, and it wasn't just me he abused. My brothers were constantly criticized by that bastard. He had three amazing, intellectually gifted sons and he treated all of them like dirt. No matter what they did, they were never good enough. It's no wonder they joined the military to make their own mark on the world."

Yeah, no wonder.

Who wouldn't want to get away from horrible parents like that?

It was a testament to their emotional strength and stubbornness that all four of the Montgomery siblings had come out of that situation sane, much less thriving as they were today.

My heart ached for Cooper, the young version and the man he was now. It couldn't have been easy growing up with zero love, support, or acceptance from his parents.

I shared that thought out loud.

"I think my brothers wanted our parents' approval when we were younger, but they eventually realized it was never going to happen," Riley mused.

"Like it wasn't already hard enough for the boys when they were sent off to boarding school because they were all intellectually gifted," Taylor said angrily.

My eyes widened. "They were?"

Being sent off to boarding school as a boy was a whole lot worse than just skipping some grades.

Harlow nodded. "Jax said he never really had a childhood. All three of them had their college degrees by the time they were eighteen."

"Cooper told me that when we met," I replied. "I just don't know a lot about his earlier life."

"I'm sure he would have told you," Riley answered. "You guys haven't really known each other for long, and really, I don't think any of us like to talk about our weird family life unless we have to for some reason. We all eventually found our closure and left all the madness behind us."

I opened my mouth to speak, but my words were cut short by my phone beeping on the table.

A few seconds later, Taylor's beeped.

And then Harlow's.

Riley laughed. "Should I be offended because I'm the only one not getting a text message? I'm pretty sure it's my brothers wondering where you all are right now."

I looked at my phone and discovered that she was right.

COOPER: *Everything okay?*

ME: *Everything is fine.*

I wanted to reach through the phone, wrap my arms around Cooper, and never let him go after hearing about his childhood.

God, no wonder he was so careful, wary, and occasionally even cynical sometimes.

COOPER: *Just checking to make sure we still have a date. I can pick you up if you've had a few drinks.*

I was perfectly sober, but I thought it was pretty sweet of him to offer.

ME: *I've only had one, and I'm perfectly able to drive. I'll probably take off from here shortly. Are you home?*

COOPER: *Just leaving the office. Wanted to see if you needed anything before I headed home.*

I sighed. Cooper Montgomery was so damn sweet.

I wasn't surprised he'd checked in to see if I needed something. I was starting to realize that doing things like that was just normal behavior for him.

Over the last week, we'd seen each other every night, and Cooper never failed to worry about whether or not I was okay.

Whether I was sleeping.

Whether I was still having nightmares.

Whether I was…happy.

He'd been a perfect gentleman. There had been no more uncontrolled, earth-shattering kisses.

I wasn't sure if I was grateful or disappointed about that.

ME: *I'm good. I'll see you soon.*

As I closed my text window, I looked around the table and saw that all three of the other women at the table were now texting on their phones.

"It was Hudson," Taylor said as she put down her phone. "Wondering how things were going."

"Same here," Harlow mentioned as she appeared to end her text conversation. "Jax was just getting worried because he thought we couldn't possibly talk this long at a happy hour. Silly man. He should know by now just how long I can hang out with the girls. He told me to take my time now that he knows we're all fine."

Riley snorted as she put her phone down. "Seth was checking on me, too. I think it's a conspiracy to separate all of us. I think the guys are getting restless and hungry. I swear they all act like they can't eat dinner without us."

"Hudson cooked," Taylor said with a laugh. "So I'm not going to complain too loudly. I guess I'd better get moving."

I looked at each of the females at the table as we gathered up our things to depart.

No matter how much they teased, it was apparent that every single one of them was gloriously happy with their significant other.

I'd never seen so many women who looked so damn eager to get home to someone who was waiting for them.

I smiled as I rose to my feet, suddenly realizing I was just as thrilled to know that someone amazing was waiting for me, too.

Chapter 14

Cooper

"That's probably the best dinner I've ever eaten," I said to Torie as we relaxed with a glass of wine at my kitchen table after dinner.

She snorted. "It was mac-n-cheese with Swedish meatballs. Nothing fancy."

"How did you know that was my favorite?" I asked her curiously.

She shrugged. "I might have questioned one of your brothers when he was at Last Hope."

Fuck! She was sweet. Women didn't do shit like that for me, so it was disarming when she went out of her way simply to...please me.

"Thank you," I said sincerely.

She swallowed a sip of her wine before she said, "It was nothing, Cooper. Not compared to all of the nice things you've done for me. Besides, I like to cook, and you even handled cleanup duty."

"I picked up a contribution to our dinner, too," I informed her.

I slid the large box I'd brought up from my downstairs fridge a few minutes ago into the center of the table.

She lifted a brow. "I have to admit that I've been curious since you brought that up."

I pulled the cake from the box and started lighting the candles.

"Oh, God," Torie moaned. "Is that an Oreo cake?"

"Chase mentioned that he and Wyatt were gone for your birthday in late October, and that it was the first time you hadn't gotten your Oreo cake. So we're celebrating your birthday." I pushed the cake toward her after all of the candles were lit. "Happy Birthday, Torie."

She put her hands to her flushed cheeks. "Oh, my God. This is insane. My birthday was a few months ago."

I shrugged. "Better to get your Oreo cake a little late than never. Make a wish and blow the candles out."

She stared at me as the light from the candles danced in her eyes. "Every year, no matter where I was, my father always made sure I had my Oreo cake for my birthday. After he died, Chase and Wyatt did the same thing. Last year, it just couldn't happen because my brothers had been away from their Paris offices for so long because of my very long recovery. They had to leave for Europe not long before my birthday. It actually means a lot that you didn't want me to miss something this sentimental."

I shrugged. "It wasn't a big deal."

She shook her head. "No, it is a big deal, Cooper. I'll make my wish, but I guarantee it will be dirty and all about you."

I coughed. "I think I'm perfectly okay with that."

Even though we didn't take any action on our attraction, we did talk or joke about it occasionally.

She smiled, took a deep breath, and blew out every candle before she asked, "How did you know where to get this? It's the same bakery my father and my brothers always used."

"I asked Chase."

My friend hadn't commented on my odd question, but I was fairly certain he'd known what I was up to when I'd asked.

"I think this thing has five thousand calories a piece," she said with a huge grin as she got up and grabbed some plates and forks. "But it's worth it."

Torie moaned through her piece of cake as I devoured two.

When she rose to get some water, I reached for the small, wrapped packaged I'd left on one of the vacant chairs so she wouldn't see it. "Birthdays shouldn't happen without a gift," I insisted as I stood and handed her the box.

"Cooper, the cake was enough," she admonished. "I don't need a gift. It's not even really my birthday."

"Humor me," I said with a grin. "It was made just for you so it's not going back."

She opened the ribbon and took off the wrapping paper. "You're insane," she said, but she was smiling. "What is it?"

"You've almost got it open," I reminded her.

When she finally had just the velvet box in her hand, she hesitated for a second before she popped it open.

"Wyatt shared that you lost your everyday jewelry that you used to wear while you were being held captive," I explained. "A necklace your father gave you, and a bracelet and earrings that your brothers gifted you for Christmas several years ago. I know your brothers replaced those earrings and your bracelet at Christmas. I know I can't even begin to replace the necklace your dad gave you, but I thought maybe I could at least give you another everyday necklace to wear."

"Oh, my God, Cooper. This is extraordinary. No necklace with this many diamonds is an everyday necklace," she said as her eyes filled with tears. "What is this?"

She'd flipped it over and was looking at the engraving on the back of the round pendant.

She fingered the words. *"De Oppresso Liber.* It's Latin. The literal translation is To Free The Oppressed."

I nodded as I lifted my shirt and turned around. I had the same words tattooed on my lower back. "It's the motto of the Army Special Forces," I explained. "I literally had those words rolling through my head for years."

I could almost hear Torie breathing as she asked, "Can I touch it? It's a beautiful tattoo."

"Yeah." Hell, she could touch any part of me that she wanted. I wasn't about to tell her she couldn't, even if the touch of her fingers on my skin made me half insane.

"Did it hurt?" she asked as she stroked a finger over the design.

I grinned. "Woman, you're asking a special forces guy if a single tattoo was painful. Even if it was, do you think I'd admit it?"

She laughed. "I'm sure you were a tough guy."

After we'd sat back down at the table, I told her, "The front of the pendant is made up of diamonds that came solely from Montgomery diamond mines. The base and the chain is platinum so it will be durable to wear every day. I guess I thought the words might resonate with you now that you're part of Last Hope and helping to free the oppressed. Because you were a hostage, I thought it might be something you'd want to keep close to your heart, too, to remind you that you're free."

"I think I'd love that. For a man who claims he's uninspired, this is probably one of the most inspired things anyone has ever done for me," she said, her voice choked with tears. "It almost seems too special to wear every day, but I will."

I rose and took the necklace from her hands and hooked it around her neck. "I'm sorry that you lost the one from your father."

"I have another one that he gave me," she explained. "But I keep it safe for special occasions. I don't want to lose it."

"Then wear this one every day," I insisted.

She bolted out of her chair the moment the necklace was secure and threw herself into my arms. "Thank you, Cooper. It's one of the most incredible gifts I've ever gotten."

I wrapped my arms around her waist and closed my eyes.

I loved the way she smelled.

I loved the way she felt.

I love the genuine sweetness in her voice.

I stroked a hand over her silky hair as she hugged me so tightly I could hardly breathe.

Not that I was complaining.

Breathing was highly overrated.

She leaned back and her eyes softened even more as she looked at me. "Riley told me a little about your family history while we were at happy hour. She mentioned what your father did to her, and how poorly your parents treated all of you. I'm so sorry you grew up that way, Cooper. No child should have parents like that. They were monsters."

"It's not like I knew that it should be any different at the time, but things should have been a hell of a lot better for Riley. If my brothers and I had known what my father had done to her before he'd died, we would have killed the bastard ourselves," I said huskily.

"I know," she acknowledged quietly. "No one can change what happened in the past, but is it wrong that I really wish that I could? You all deserved so much better."

I closed my eyes for a second to try to get my dick under control.

I couldn't have this gorgeous woman this close to me without my brain going places that it really shouldn't.

"It's over," I told her. "All of us decided a long time ago that we weren't going to give either of our parents another moment of our lives. They took enough from us, especially Riley."

Torie held me tighter and buried her face against my neck.

I sensed that she was actually trying to comfort me somehow, and just the fact that she wanted to do that made my damn chest ache.

"It was a long time ago, Torie," I said hoarsely as I ran my hands up and down her back.

"Maybe so," she said in a muffled voice against my skin. "But I still hate it for you. For all of you. When did you ever get to be a child, Cooper? It's hard enough for a kid to grow up different, to start skipping grades and never have the same friends for very long because of that. I had the support of my parents and my brothers. You had no one to guide you except your brothers, and I'm sure they had their share of confusion, too."

"Don't," I told her adamantly. "It was a long time ago, sweetheart. None of us had a childhood, but we're all okay now. That's all that really matters."

"Do you have any idea what an amazing man you are, Cooper Montgomery?" she asked earnestly.

Hell, no, I didn't, and I wasn't.

I shook my head. "I'm not. You just don't know me very well yet."

She tugged on my hair gently. "Stop that," she insisted. "Don't mock yourself like that, and don't you dare blow off the fact that you're incredible."

"If you want to believe that, I'm not about to argue," I agreed, mesmerized by the sight of her beautiful lips as she said those fierce words.

Fuck! I wanted to kiss her, even though I knew I shouldn't.

I also wanted to be that incredible man she thought I was, that guy worth keeping.

"Good, then don't argue," she said happily as she pulled my head down and fused our mouths together, saving me the agony of trying to decide whether or not I should kiss her.

I devoured her lips, but almost immediately, I knew that wasn't going to be enough.

I needed more.

I wanted too damn much.

And I couldn't seem to stop myself from feeling all of those emotions.

Fuck! I wanted both of us naked. Nothing between the two of us.

Torie was an ache that I didn't think I could ever assuage.

The one woman who could definitely bring me to my knees without really trying.

I groaned and pulled my lips away from hers. "Christ, Torie. You're killing me," I growled.

"I don't want to kill you," she whispered as she put her hands under my shirt to touch my bare skin. "I just want to touch you, Cooper."

Jesus Christ!

Fucking hell!

And every other curse word I could think of at the moment.

I *wanted* her hands all over me.

Just. Like. This.

Okay. Yeah. I'd had some decent sex in my life, but nothing in my past had ever felt this damn good, and we weren't even close to the main event.

"Cooper," Torie moaned. "I need you. Please."

And…I felt like a fucking god just because she wanted me.

I buried my face against her neck and started to devour the soft skin there. "Easy, sweetheart," I warned. "If we don't stop, you might get way more than you could possibly want right now."

Hell, I didn't just want to fuck Torie.

I wanted her to be mine in every possible way.

The last thing I wanted was for her to back off because I pushed her too far, too fast.

She trusted me, goddammit!

Fuck! I have to stop!

"I want you, Cooper," Torie panted.

I claimed her lips so she couldn't say another word.

If she did, I knew I'd have her naked before I could stop myself.

Chapter 15

Torie

I could feel Cooper's hesitance, and I wasn't sure what to do. I'd never wanted to be with a man as much as I wanted Cooper Montgomery, but I needed that intense desire to go both ways.

I couldn't do this any other way. I couldn't let him get me naked unless we were both fully engaged.

I had too many scars.

I had too many lingering fears.

I was going to need him to be all in with me.

It took everything I had to wrench my mouth from his and step back.

Sweet Jesus! What in the hell am I thinking?

I'd been the one to start this intense kiss when he'd obviously wanted to slow things down.

"Maybe all of this *is* happening too fast," I panted.

For a moment, I felt truly panicked, and I started to hyperventilate. Everything with Cooper had been so damn perfect.

Until it wasn't.

What exactly had happened?

Cooper put an arm around my waist. "Take it easy, baby. Breathe."

"I'm breathing," I said shakily.

"No, you're not," he said patiently. "Breathe."

I took a deep breath in.

Cooper and I were supposed to be casual dating.

Casual. Dating.

For me, that term had never meant a rambunctious fuck on the kitchen table with someone who wasn't in a committed relationship with me.

Dammit! There was just something about Cooper Montgomery that made every rational thought fly out of my head.

And that was saying something since I had a genius IQ, but apparently very little common sense at the moment.

"You're really upset. What in the hell did I do, Torie?" Cooper asked in a hoarse, raspy voice right next to my ear. "Tell me what in the hell I did and I'll fix it."

He turned me around until I was facing him.

My breath caught as I looked up to see the troubled look in his eyes.

I slowly shook my head. "It's nothing you did, Cooper. It was me. I got ridiculously carried away. I shouldn't have even initiated a crazy kiss like that."

"Hey," he said gently. "I think there were two of us involved. Jesus, Torie, it's not like I didn't want exactly what you did. Please don't tell me that you're under the impression that I don't want you as much as you want me."

I absolutely did think that he'd been hesitant.

I'd felt it.

I nodded. "Maybe I do think that. God, I didn't mean to push things, Cooper. You're probably the most amazing guy I've ever met. We're friends, and we're just supposed to be casual dating."

He shook his head. "Don't. Don't for one single second believe that I didn't want to get you naked and fuck you until you begged for mercy. But that's just not going to happen until you're ready. That's a big hurdle for you to get over, Torie, and I get that. You have to be able to trust me. Our attraction isn't going to be enough. One step at a time, sweetheart. I'm not planning on going anywhere. Now tell me how you're feeling now that you're breathing."

"I'm fine."

He shook his head as he swiped a tear from my cheek. "You're crying, and they're definitely not happy tears."

I shrugged. "Okay, then maybe I'm a mess. Maybe I have been since my nightmares came back. I'm not myself, Cooper. I'm so tired that my emotions are all over the place."

"The new therapy with Dr. Romero isn't helping?" he asked gruffly.

"I'm not quite sure yet. We've only met once so far. I'm sure it will help, but over the last week, I've had nightmares almost every night. I think I'm suffering from pure exhaustion," I admitted reluctantly.

"Why in the hell didn't you call me?" he asked.

"I can't call you every time I have a bad dream, Cooper. You'd be as sleep deprived as I am right now."

I was having a meltdown, and I knew it, but Cooper was my safe place to fall.

Even though the time I spent with Cooper made me ecstatically happy, my nightmares and my lack of sleep were starting to weigh on me pretty heavily.

My sleep deprivation was starting to win the battle for my mental wellbeing.

Cooper wrapped his arms around me and held me tightly against his body. "I'm sorry, sweetheart. We'll figure this all out and find a way to beat it. From now on, you call me if you have a nightmare."

I wrapped my arms around his neck, and for once, I allowed myself to lean on someone. "I'm just so damn tired, Cooper."

He kneeled at my feet and meticulously took off both of my sandals.

"Then stay," he demanded as he straightened up again. "Stay here with me, Torie. Maybe it will help if you have someone right next to you in case you need them. No strings. No pressure. Nothing sexual. Just a warm body to keep you company."

His offer was so damn tempting that I groaned aloud. "Cooper, I can't do that. I don't have any of my things here right now—"

"We'll get some of your things tomorrow," he said insistently as he scooped me up into his arms. "I might be attracted to you, but your mental health is a hell of a lot more important to me right now, Torie. You have to sleep. You can't continue to function this way."

I wrapped my arms around his neck. "I know. I'm not sure what to do. I'm not this woman who's this unsure of myself. I'm not this woman who cries at the drop of a hat. I hate what the kidnapping has done to my head. I was doing okay until the nightmares came back—"

"This isn't your fault, baby. Everything will be okay. You just need more time."

I sighed as he stepped into an elevator. "I wish I could be as sure of that as you are," I replied.

He entered his master suite and gently sat me on the bed before he went to his walk-in closet. "For now, you can wear one of my T-shirts to bed. You can bring whatever you want in the morning. For right now, my physical desires are on hold, Torie. All I want is to help you sleep. I can't fucking stand to see you like this."

A few minutes later, I exited the big master bathroom in one of Cooper's T-shirts.

He glanced at me from his position on the bed and grinned. "That shirt looks a hell of a lot better on you that it ever looked on me."

"You can see nearly every scar on my body," I said in a hushed voice.

I had so many injuries, so many scars.

He shook his head. "All I see is the most courageous woman I've ever known."

My eyes teared up because I knew he meant that. I could tell by the way he was looking at me right now.

He didn't see my scars.

He didn't see my imperfections.

He didn't blame me for having a major meltdown from lack of sleep.

The garment was soft with age and was obviously well-worn. "Thanks for this," I said as I slipped between the sheets next to Cooper.

Even if this didn't help me sleep any better, I was touched that he was willing to try it.

I breathed in Cooper's irresistible scent as I tried to get comfortable. The king-size bed was enormous, and the sheets were ridiculously soft. But I just wasn't used to sleeping with someone. I hadn't had a serious boyfriend in a long time.

"Come here," he said in a comforting baritone right after he'd turned off the light.

He wrapped a strong arm around my waist and pulled my body against his. "Relax, sweetheart," he instructed as he stroked a soothing hand over my hair.

I allowed myself to unwind and calm down as I put my head on his shoulder.

Just knowing that Cooper would be right here if I woke up completely terrified from one of my nightmares was comforting.

"What happens if this does work?" I asked as my eyes grew heavy.

Cooper continued to stroke his hand over my hair as he said mischievously, "Then I suppose you're stuck sleeping in my bed for the rest of your life. I'd have to be an idiot to complain about that."

I smiled as my eyes fluttered closed.

I very much doubted whether I'd have a single problem with that arrangement myself.

Chapter 16

Cooper

The next two weeks were a strange combination of the happiest days of my life and pure hell.

I was elated because Torie was practically living at my place, and her nightmares had started to slow down significantly.

They still happened, but she was usually able to go back to sleep within a few minutes, so she was completely rested every day.

However, spending every single night with her soft, curvy body plastered on top of mine was almost more than a guy could possibly endure.

Despite that fact, I'd done my best to ignore my baser urges for the sake of Torie's mental health.

Yeah, being this damn close to her and not wanting more was difficult, but I'd learned one thing over the last two weeks: I couldn't do a sexual relationship with Torie while we were "casual dating."

Fuck no!

I had to know that she was committed to an exclusive relationship.

There was no possible way I could fuck her and not know that she wasn't going to date anyone else. Like…ever.

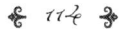

I'd lose my mind just like my two older brothers if I couldn't make Torie mine.

There was absolutely nothing casual in the way I felt about Torie, so I was willing to wait until she was ready to commit to something exclusive.

Right now, all I wanted was for her to feel like she was whole again.

The more time we spent together, the more I realized how badly her kidnapping had not only messed with her body, but her head, too.

She'd tried to put on a brave face for her brothers, but inside, Torie was still wrestling with some of her more persistent demons.

Over time, she'd opened up with my promise that I'd never tell her brothers.

To be honest, I could understand why there were some things she didn't want to tell Chase and Wyatt.

Her kidnappers had been even crueler and more sociopathic than she'd ever revealed to her brothers after her kidnapping. Chase and Wyatt had known things were bad because of her injuries, but it was worse than they ever could have imagined. The head games those bastards had played with Torie were fucked up and her captors had gotten off on her fear and her pain. I had no doubt that hearing every single detail of Torie's ordeal would probably kill Chase and Wyatt.

Hell, every revelation she made haunted me, but I tried like hell to separate my emotions from her pain because Torie needed someone she could talk to about everything.

I was determined to be that confidante, even if it nearly destroyed me to hear about what they'd done to her.

It was no wonder she was still struggling, that she hadn't completely found her way back to normal…yet.

"What's the plan for today?" a sleepy Torie whispered next to my ear.

Fucking hell. Did she always have to wake up sounding like a damn seductress in the morning?

As usual, she'd managed to crawl on top of me during the night, one leg over my thighs, her head on top of my chest, that gorgeous mane of light brown hair spread out over my skin, and those luscious damn breasts pressed against my ribs.

Also, as usual, I had my arms wrapped around her body, trying to bring her even closer so I could up my suffering factor.

Christ! I really was a masochist.

Torie got cold when she was asleep and she wrapped her body around me at night like I was a warm blanket.

Hell, not that I was complaining, but it was pretty fucking difficult not to wake up hard and ready to go when this happened every single morning.

"I thought we could do the Eagle Park hike if you're up for it. Or we could just go kayaking in the cove. It's supposed to hit seventy degrees today," I said, trying like hell not to focus on how damn good she felt exactly where she was right now.

"I'm up for Eagle Park," she said hastily. "It's winter, and the water is still cold. But Eagle Park isn't exactly a challenge for you. None of our hikes have been so far."

I opened my mouth to ask her why she shied away every time I mentioned doing anything even remotely close to the water. And then I closed it again.

Torie always shared what she was comfortable telling me.

She'd been born and raised in San Diego.

She snorkeled and was certified for scuba, so I knew she didn't have a natural aversion to the ocean.

Whatever her issue was with the water, I knew it had something to do with her time in captivity in the Amazon.

"It's a longer hike," I reminded her. "Does it really matter how challenging it is if we're getting outside for the day?"

I'd picked our hikes carefully, slowly working up to longer excursions. Torie might be an expert hiker, but it wasn't like she could just jump back into long distance hiking like she used to do.

Honestly, the way she'd fallen back into hitting the trails amazed me. She was probably capable of more difficult hikes, but I saw no reason to rush things.

"It doesn't matter to me," she said as she raised her head and met my gaze. "I just don't want you to get bored."

Hell, like that was even possible?

Every moment I spent with Torie was a learning experience.

I'd dated.

I'd fucked.

But I'd never really experienced having a woman in my life who actually seemed to want nothing more than to spend time with me. I'd never really understood how intimate it could be to have a female in my life who was definitely a friend, but could also turn my body inside out with carnal thoughts about her, too.

"No possible way I could be bored when I'm with you," I told her honestly as I ran my fingers through her hair, which was a morning habit I couldn't seem to kick.

Torie wore her hair in a big, thick braid most of the time when she was hiking or doing anything physical because the thick mass of waves got in her way. But when that glorious mane was set free, it was one of the sexiest things I'd ever seen or felt before.

She pressed her palm against my cheek. "Thank you for all of this. I kind of just barged into your entire life and you accepted that to try to tame my nightmares. I'm really not sure quite what to do now that the nightmares are starting to get better. I think I'm safe to go back to my condo tonight, Cooper. Between your warm body and my intensive therapy, my nightmares aren't interrupting my sleep anymore. I feel fantastic now that I'm sleeping normally again."

Oh, hell no.

I shook my head. "Not yet. You aren't disrupting my life. I want you here. I think it's too soon to make any changes that could bring those nightmares back in full force all over again, Torie."

She slipped her leg off my body and moved to my side. "What guy actually likes a woman who uses him like a heating pad?"

Fucking hell.

Torie Durand could use me any way she wanted and I'd be perfectly content.

As long as she was happy.

"Have you heard me objecting?" I asked as I tightened an arm around her.

She wasn't going anywhere until we worked this whole sleeping arrangement out.

Torie turned until her front was plastered against my side. "No," she admitted with a sigh. "But then, you're a pretty extraordinary man."

I gritted my teeth as she ran a soft hand over my stomach. No doubt it was almost an unconscious, affectionate move for her, but it was fucking torture for me.

Yet, I didn't want her to stop touching me like that, either.

Fuck! I definitely must like tormenting myself and I probably needed some kind of treatment for that sooner rather than later.

"I'm extraordinary because I don't mind having a beautiful woman in my bed?" I asked gruffly.

She snorted. "It's not like you take advantage of that fact, and it's not like you haven't seen most of my scars by now. But take my word for it, the areas you haven't seen don't look any better. My body's not exactly a pretty sight."

She'd said that a hundred times, but there was nothing about her scars that made her any less attractive. Not to me. The only thing that really bothered me was how much pain she'd been put through to gain that many scars.

"You're gorgeous, and don't think that I haven't been tempted to take advantage," I informed her roughly as I rolled her over on her back and stared down at her face. "Jesus, Torie! Do you really think that this has been easy for me?"

I started to drown in her mesmerizing, amber-eyed gaze as she shook her head slowly, her eyes never leaving mine. "Probably not," she said softly. "But you're still here, and you still want me to be here with you. I find that extraordinary."

"Because I fucking want to help you," I growled. "What's going on in your head is more important than a pair of blue balls."

"Oh, Cooper," she said with a soft sigh as she threaded her fingers into my hair. "Do you have any idea how few men there are like you out there?"

"I doubt that," I said, blowing off her compliment. "I'm sure there are plenty of blue-balled bastards out there."

I didn't think I was an exception.

Most guys would give a shit if they cared about their woman at all.

I leaned down and kissed her, unable to go another second without some kind of connection to her.

She responded with a tiny moan against my lips as she wrapped her arms around my neck.

I lost track of just how long that embrace went on, but I was careful not to let it get too carnal.

For now, just being close to Torie was going to have to be enough.

"Cooper," she said in a breathy, fuck-me voice as I finally released her lips.

It nearly killed me.

She wanted.

I needed to satisfy.

That's just the kind of chemistry that constantly flowed from her to me every minute of the day, and it was pure hell not to immediately respond to any kind of signal from her.

Problem was, Torie was also vulnerable right now, and my instinct to protect her was constantly at war with my need to sink my cock inside her.

I closed my eyes, trying to ignore the battle, and kissed her soundly on the forehead. "Time to get up, beautiful. The day is waiting."

I rolled my ass out of bed before I could give in to my baser instincts to spend the entire day burning up the sheets with Torie instead.

Chapter 17

Torie

"This was such an amazing day," I told Cooper right after I'd devoured the last of my lobster ravioli.

After we'd tackled the Eagle Park trail, Cooper and I had cleaned up at his place, and at his insistence, we'd just finished dinner at a local Italian restaurant in La Jolla.

Although we'd fallen into a routine of eating at home some of the time, both of us still enjoyed our food and we grabbed takeout or ate at a restaurant whenever we felt like it.

Those occurrences happened fairly often since Cooper seemed to love to take me out, especially on the weekends.

"How was the lobster ravioli?" he asked as he nodded at my empty plate.

"Fabulous," I said with a sigh. "Anything with a carb count that high is naturally going to be my friend."

He chuckled. "I think you worked off the calories today."

I nodded as I smiled at him. "It feels fantastic to get back out on the trails again. I'll work my way back up to the expert hikes, eventually."

At some point, I was bound to crave something more challenging, but for now, I was enjoying my intermediate jaunts with Cooper.

Maybe it was my hiking partner that made these trips so special. In the past, most of my hiking was a solitary sport. It felt so different to actually share what I was discovering on my hikes with someone like Cooper.

He lifted a brow as he sat back in his chair. "Just remember that you promised to take me with you if you decide to hijack my jet."

I laughed. "Now that I'm living back in San Diego, I could probably commandeer one of my brother's jets. When they're not in Europe, there's usually one of them sitting at the airport."

"No need," he answered. "Mine is always there unless we're using it for a mission or I'm at a mining site, which rarely happens anymore since we have good executives who do a lot of the traveling for us these days."

I took a sip of my wine while I studied his face. "So, just like that? I can borrow your jet whenever I want it?"

Dating or not, what billionaire offered a woman from a casual dating relationship free access to his private jet?

He shrugged. "Why not? It's not like I use it all the time."

"I am capable of getting a charter?" I reminded him.

He shook his head adamantly. "Don't. You never know how the maintenance has been on a charter jet. Mine is safer."

I nearly choked on my wine, but it wasn't the first time that Cooper had said something outrageous when it came to my wellbeing.

No matter how rational or matter-of-fact Cooper might be, his brain didn't function quite that way when it came to the people he cared about.

"I doubt I'm going to need that jet in the near future," I answered wistfully. "I don't think I'm quite ready to take on any international challenges right now."

It hadn't been easy for me to admit that I needed more help than I'd thought was necessary to get over what had happened to me in the Amazon.

In some ways, I'd been in denial because all I'd wanted was for those memories to go away so things could go back to normal for me.

They didn't.

And they wouldn't.

Not until I'd worked through all of that trauma.

Granted, I felt so much better since I'd started therapy with Dr. Romero and I'd started sleeping more normally at night.

I felt more like myself again, but I wasn't completely there yet.

I wasn't ready to go out and conquer the entire world, but maybe I could overcome one piece at a time.

"You will be ready for that, Torie," Cooper said in a husky tone. "Cut yourself some breaks. You nearly died in the Amazon. It took months to heal from your physical injuries before you could even begin to tackle the emotional ones. You'll be out there traveling the world again before you know it."

His last sentence sounded slightly pained, like he wasn't all that excited about the idea of me traveling the planet. "I'm not so sure that I'll ever quite be the same woman I was before," I mused. "I think traveling will always be part of my life, but I was already planning on slowing my travel down a year ago. After my father died, I started to understand just how short life could be. I didn't want to live so far away from my brothers anymore. Not that they've bothered to make me an auntie yet, but I hope they will. If not, at least we'll see each other more often unless they're in Paris."

"So you were already planning your move back to San Diego?" Cooper asked.

I nodded. "I was already thinking about it. San Diego is home for me. I liked living in New York, but I think I always knew I'd eventually find my way home."

"Not that I like the way that it happened," Cooper said huskily. "But I'm glad you're here. Chase and Wyatt mentioned you fairly often."

I nodded. "They talked about you and your brothers to me, too. I just never really understood how you'd all gotten so close. I guess I just assumed you'd met through business connections. My brothers were as forthcoming with me about Last Hope as you and your brothers have been with Riley."

Cooper shrugged. "It's not that we didn't trust Riley," he explained. "There was just never any real reason for her to know. She worried herself to death when all of us were in special forces. We didn't want to put her through that again."

"I guess I can understand that," I murmured. "I worried about Chase and Wyatt, too. But aren't you afraid that you'll slip up someday? Last Hope is an important part of your lives. It's the way that your brothers met Taylor and Harlow."

"Those two did share the information about their kidnapping with Riley, so it's not like she doesn't know about it," Cooper explained. "My little sister just has no idea that Hudson and Jax were the men who actually rescued them."

I folded my arms over my chest. "Do you really think it's fair that she's the only one who's in the dark about Last Hope? Just like Chase and Wyatt, you and your brothers mostly do the financing and strategic planning these days, so she won't exactly have to fret much if you tell her now."

"We can't tell her," Cooper said adamantly.

"Why not?" I challenged.

Cooper drained his wine glass before he answered. "If you really must know, she'd probably kill all three of us for lying to her for so long. Years ago, when Last Hope was smaller, and we ran the missions ourselves, we used to tell Riley that we were treasure hunters, and that's why we were out of the country so much. That was Jax's idea, and he got pretty carried away with his stories about our supposed exploits around the world. Do you have any idea how pissed off she'd be that we've been making that shit up for years now?"

I shot him a startled look before I finally started to laugh. "Oh, my God. None of you are willing to tell her because you know she probably won't speak to you for weeks over it."

"Pretty much," he said reluctantly. "Riley can hold a grudge for a long time when she feels like it."

I knew it was true, but I was having a hard time accepting the fact that three alpha male billionaires were actually terrified of their little sister's reaction about them lying to her.

"So what happens if she finds out years down the line?" I questioned. "You don't think she'll be even more hurt? Since every single one of you knows about Last Hope, the information is bound to slip someday."

"We try not to think about it, and we're all damn careful."

"I honestly think you should just rip the Band-Aid off and tell her. She'd never tell anyone, and if my brothers had fallen in love and everyone knew about Last Hope except me, I think I'd feel a little… betrayed," I said thoughtfully.

"It's a secret group—"

"A secret private group," I corrected. "It's not like you'd be revealing military or government secrets. She's your sister, Cooper."

He shot me a disgruntled look. "Taylor and Harlow have been saying the same thing. Both of them are afraid they'll slip someday, and all three of them have gotten pretty close."

"Really close," I agreed. "Do you have any idea how upset Taylor or Harlow will be if they mention Last Hope by accident to Riley? They'd be devastated if they were the ones to hurt her."

We'd spent an entire Sunday with Cooper's family at a barbecue, and I'd had to watch every word I said because I didn't want to spill the beans to Riley.

"Fuck! You're probably right," he rasped. "I'll talk to Hudson and Jax. Maybe it's not fair to ask Taylor and Harlow to keep lying about it forever."

"For what it's worth," I said. "I wasn't overly upset with Chase and Wyatt for never mentioning it, but things change when other people and friendships become involved and that lie keeps getting bigger."

He nodded. "You're right. I guess my main concern was protecting Riley."

"I can hardly fault you for that," I assured him. "I just thought I'd bring up a different perspective since I've been that little sister since the day I was born, too. We're much tougher than you think.

Riley might be hurt initially, but she knows not a single one of you would ever want to hurt her."

He shot me a dubious glance. "You have no idea how unforgiving she can be. I love my little sister but she can be an unrelenting, red-headed menace with the hottest temper you've ever seen."

"She loves all of you, too, and she'll eventually get over it," I reassured him.

"Remember that you said that when she's throwing a fit over it someday," he said unhappily.

I hid my smile behind my wineglass as I dropped the subject.

I had no doubt that Cooper and his brothers would eventually do the right thing. They cared too much about their sister, Harlow, and Taylor to resolve the situation any other way.

Chapter 18

Cooper

"She's doing better," I told my brothers the next day. "But something's still not right. I don't know what the hell to do."

The three of us needing to come into the office on a Sunday was rare, but I was suddenly glad that we were able to talk in the conference room after our business meeting was over.

We'd decided to order up lunch since Harlow, Taylor, and Torie were at Jax's place making some plans for Taylor's wedding.

Jax reached into one of the bags on the table and pulled out his burger. "Honestly, you'd never know that Torie was still struggling. She hides it really well. What do you think is going on?"

I shook my head as I chewed and swallowed a bite of my cheeseburger. "I'm not sure. Something's still not quite right, which probably isn't surprising considering how much pleasure those assholes took in hurting her."

Torie was sleeping again.

She smiled a lot more often.

Her therapy with Dr. Romero was working to help her PTSD and her nightmares.

She talked about nearly everything that had happened to her. But something was still…off.

"Why didn't you tell us she was staying with you?" Hudson asked. "And why didn't you come to us when you found out she was struggling with trauma after her kidnapping?"

I shrugged. My brothers weren't stupid. Once they'd realized Torie was staying with me, they'd asked what was going on, so I'd told them about her nightmares. "I promised I wouldn't tell her brothers about the bad dreams. I guess I never thought about the fact that both of you have been through all this before."

Jax lifted a brow. "So are you done telling us we've lost our minds?"

I nodded. "Yeah. I get it. There is no reasoning with a man when he's crazy about a woman. I'm there. That's why I'm asking for your help. She's hurting, and I fucking hate it. I don't know what else I can do."

"Be there for her, Coop," Hudson advised solemnly. "It's a helpless goddamn feeling when there is really nothing you can do. We want to fix it, but we can't. Not with all the money in the world. Just stay with her and don't let her back away. And for fuck's sake, don't back away from her, either. I worried about pushing Taylor too soon because my emotions were running rampant over what had happened to her. Those efforts caused more problems than they helped. Torie is a strong woman. She'll get through all of this. Just be there to support her."

"It really hasn't been all that long," Jax added. "And in Torie's case, she had to heal some extreme bodily injuries before she could even start to think about getting her head straight."

"That's what I told her," I said roughly. "She's seeing Dr. Romero, and I think that's helping. Fuck! Maybe I'm just impatient because I hate hearing her criticize herself. She's the most incredible woman I've ever met, but she's still not happy with her progress. She almost never cuts herself a damn break."

"Then you be there to remind her that she needs to take it easy on herself," Jax advised. "Harlow did the same thing. She was critical about every damn thing she did during and after the kidnapping. It took her a long time to realize that just escaping with her life was a fucking miracle."

Hudson tossed his burger wrapper into one of the empty bags and leaned back in his chair. "I take it you're going to be in this relationship for the long haul?" he asked.

"And then some," I rasped. "I'm sorry for every stupid thing I ever said about romantic relationships. Not that I would trade the way I feel about Torie, but I wish I would have realized that losing my mind was going to be inevitable if I met the right woman. I didn't get it. I didn't understand what both of you were going through, and I'm sorry for that. Christ! It hurts like hell when she's hurting. It's like we feel the same fucking pain."

I had no doubt it was the same way for Hudson and Jax.

Hudson shrugged. "I'm not sure it's possible to comprehend until it happens to you. How can any guy imagine that they'd wake up one day and one woman would become their everything? That one single female could make or break their entire life."

"Fuck!" I cursed. "How in the hell is a guy supposed to live through this? It's torture."

Jax grinned. "It gets better. It's only difficult until you realize that having the right woman can make you the happiest bastard in the world, too. It might be painful and confusing in the beginning, but it's worth it."

"Definitely worth it," Hudson agreed.

I slammed my fist down on the table as I growled, "You better tell me how to get through the hard part of this first, because I feel like I'm losing my shit."

I wasn't comforted as Hudson and Jax exchanged a knowing look before Jax said, "I can make things easy for you, but I doubt you'll listen."

"Tell me," I insisted.

"Number one. Admit from the very beginning that you have absolutely no control," Jax said as he held up a single finger.

"Number two," he continued as he held up a second finger. "Don't try to fight any of it."

"And number three," he said as he held up a third finger. "Nail her ass down to a committed relationship as soon as possible. It helps when you know she's already yours. After that, it's just a matter of working out the details."

I eyed Jax suspiciously before I looked at Hudson.

"He's right," Hudson confirmed. "Half the pain is not knowing how to make her yours or how to make her happy."

I snorted. "Fuck! If I had those things figured out, I wouldn't be asking for your help. I have no idea how she really feels about me. The chemistry between the two of us has always been there, but I need a hell of a lot more than to just get laid. Technically, we're *still* casually dating."

Hudson shook his head adamantly. "Oh, hell no. That shit is dangerous."

"We're friends, too," I added.

"Even worse," Jax said with a frown. "You can't really believe that being relegated to the friend zone is going to work in this situation, right? Because I can already tell that it will make you completely insane."

"Tried that?" I guessed.

"And failed miserably," Jax finished.

"I've been waiting for her to decide when she's ready to move to something more serious," I groaned.

"I have a feeling she's already tried to tell you what she wants but you probably weren't listening," Jax mused. "Most likely, she's clueless."

"That's not possible," I said through gritted teeth.

"Nah. It's definitely possible," Hudson assured me. "Somewhere you two got your wires crossed. Look, Coop, you have to go after what you want. I'm not saying to run her ass over, but be clear about what you want and in what time frame you see that happening. She's the one who's still trying to get over her issues. Don't confuse the crap out of her."

"I'm not," I informed him. "At least, I don't think that I am."

"If you're not sure, she probably isn't, either," Jax said thoughtfully. "Check in with her. Make sure you know what she wants. No pressure, but if you screw this one up, you probably won't get another chance. We all waited over thirty years to feel this way the first time."

"Glad there's no pressure," I said in an ornery tone.

"Neither one of us is trying to be a smart-ass," Hudson told me. "We're just telling you the truth. And as far as helping her goes, there isn't a whole lot you can do, Cooper. Listen to her when she wants to talk, and just be with her when she doesn't. Jax and I both know that shit eats your guts out. When you care that much about someone, their pain really does become yours."

"All I want is to make her happy," I confessed, feeling helplessly inept.

"The stakes are a lot higher for you than they were a year ago with Fiona," Hudson drawled.

"Do you think I don't know that?" I asked tightly. "I never expected to meet someone like Torie. I didn't know it was possible for a woman to turn my whole life upside down. I've tried every mind trick I can think of to keep from making a total ass of myself in front of her. To slow things down just in case she doesn't want the same things I do. I don't know how to fucking keep that shit up."

We slept in the same goddamn bed every night and I was running out of patience and excuses as to why we shouldn't be burning up the sheets every damn night.

She wanted me.

Fuck knew I wanted her.

Wouldn't we both feel better if we let ourselves drown in carnal bliss?

"Jesus, Coop, you need to really talk to her. Does it really matter if you make an ass out of yourself if the end result is Torie being yours?" Hudson asked firmly.

"No. It doesn't matter," I told him, being completely honest with him. "I'd make myself an idiot to the entire world if I thought it would bring the two of us closer. I guess I'm afraid that…it won't."

"But it might," Jax countered. "You've spent your entire life being the rational brother, Cooper. Your scholastic gifts have always been your reasoning ability, that lightning fast skill to evaluate every outcome and come up with the right answer. Things have always had to make sense to you. Love just doesn't work that way, little brother. There's rarely a correct answer, and taking a leap of faith quite frequently involves some pain along the way because you don't always get a soft landing."

Hudson nodded. "You'll probably have to take some risks that will never make sense to your reasonable brain."

"I've never been a risk taker. You know that," I reminded them. "I've never had to be. I'm not saying that I'm not willing when it comes to Torie. There isn't much I wouldn't do to make her happy."

"That's all you really need to know," Jax explained. "It's trial and error from here to figure out what will make her happy. She cares about you, Coop. It's obvious whenever I see you two together. I know what it feels like to want to make all of her pain go away, and I know how frustrating it is when you can't sometimes. Try to be patient. You're helping just by being there for her, even though it doesn't feel like it."

I nodded, eager to change the subject as I looked at Hudson and asked, "Do you think they have your wedding planned yet?"

"Christ! I hope so," he answered adamantly. "These have been the longest months of my life. I was ready to get married the minute I proposed."

Jax snickered, but for once, I knew exactly how Hudson felt.

Chapter 19

Torie

"I think it's going to be a beautiful wedding," I told Taylor and Harlow in a wistful voice. "It doesn't matter which venue you pick."

The three of us had spent much of the morning surfing through possible venues and gathering as much info as possible so Taylor could make a final choice.

We'd finally taken a break, the three of us simply taking up space on Jax's living room floor now that our work was done.

Taylor smiled radiantly. "Hudson will be relieved when I finally set a date and get our venue. It's hard to believe he actually thinks I'll dump him before the wedding or something."

"He's insecure?" I questioned.

She nodded. "Can you imagine?"

"Jax is, too," Harlow shared. "I'll never understand why a guy like Jax has any insecurities."

I cocked my head as I looked at Harlow and Taylor. "You don't think they should be insecure because they're rich and powerful guys?"

They both nodded as Harlow added, "Not to mention the fact that they're both incredibly hot."

"Being rich doesn't give a person a pass in the insecurity department," I said drily. "I can attest to that personally. We're as human as the next person."

"How are things going with you and Cooper?" Harlow asked curiously. "Are the nightmares still bothering you?"

I'd gotten to know both of these women better since we'd first met for happy hour. I talked to them both by phone and text, and seeing them at Hudson's barbecue had felt like greeting old friends, even though we weren't.

The more I got to know them, the more I felt comfortable talking to them.

Maybe we'd bonded over the fact that we were all former captives in a kidnapping, but we had a lot more in common than that.

"The nightmares are better," I shared. "And I'm not sure how things are going with Cooper. I'm not always sure what he's thinking sometimes, and it's still not all that easy to sleep with a man like him and not think about doing more than sleeping. But I wouldn't trade our relationship for anything. He is the most incredible guy I've ever known."

"He can be a hard man to read sometimes," Harlow agreed. "I was a little intimated by him when we first met."

"Ditto," Taylor said. "He's so damn smart that he's scary sometimes. He's the only person, male or female, that can completely kick my ass at chess. Not that I've given up trying, but Cooper is always several steps ahead of me, and I was taught by a world champion. Honestly, I think Cooper could take any of the current champions, but he doesn't seem to care about besting anyone. He just likes to play the game."

I shook my head. "I didn't know he played that well."

"I'm not surprised," Taylor remarked. "Cooper isn't exactly the kind of guy who brags about his talents."

No, he wasn't, which just made him that much more intriguing.

He'd asked me if I played once, but he'd never suggested a game when I'd said that I did play a game occasionally with my brothers.

No doubt our chess game would be over in a heartbeat if Cooper was as good as Taylor said. My chess skills were mediocre at best.

"Cooper is cautious," Harlow mused. "But once you get to know him, he's also incredibly kind. He's crazy about you, Torie. I can tell by the way he looks at you. Even when he's talking to someone else, his gaze is never far away from you."

I shook my head. "I'm not sure what to think. I essentially threw myself at him a couple of times, and he backed off. We both did, actually, and things have never gotten quite that hot and heavy again. Maybe that's a good thing since we're still just casually dating. It's not like we're an exclusive item."

"No way," Harlow said softly. "He never looks ready to back away when I see the two of you together. He looks like he wants to swallow you whole."

"I wish," I said quietly.

"No," Taylor said. "She's right. What makes you think he doesn't want you?"

"We sleep in the same bed every night and things have never gone further than kissing," I said drily.

Harlow frowned. "But don't you think he's doing that for you? Because you're still having nightmares and some other issues from your kidnapping."

Harlow, Taylor, and Riley all knew that I'd been sexually assaulted during my kidnapping. In fact, it had really helped to have some conversations with Taylor since she'd gone through the same thing.

"I'm not sure," I replied uncertainly. "I've done everything but get naked in front of him to give Cooper the green light. I'm ready. God, I couldn't even think about another man. Not when I've got someone like Cooper right there in front of me. I'd have to be crazy not to want him."

"Wouldn't be the first time," Taylor considered. "He's been dumped before."

Wait. She was right. Cooper has been dumped before.

"By someone who only wanted his money," I agreed. "A female that ridiculous doesn't count."

"But it hurts just as much," Harlow said. "He's insecure, just like Hudson and Jax can be. I don't think it's that he doesn't want you, Torie. I think he's more afraid that you don't want him. Or that he'll do something that will ruin your relationship. More than likely, he doesn't want to rush you because of all the abuse you took in the Amazon."

"That's crazy," I sputtered. "Not even possible. Cooper Montgomery is every woman's fantasy. But you might be right about his fear of rushing me. Although I have no idea how he could have missed about a thousand green lights from me lately."

Taylor lifted a brow. "Obviously, he isn't every woman's fantasy if he's been dumped in the past. I think you need to seduce him."

I actually giggled at the thought. "I missed every single one of my seductress lessons."

"Believe me," Harlow said drily. "I doubt it would take much judging by the way he looks at you when you're together."

"Do you really think it's possible that he thinks *I'm* still hesitant?"

"Absolutely," Harlow and Taylor said at the same time.

Taylor continued, "He knows you've been through a lot, and if he's anything like his brothers, he's going to be afraid to push too hard. I think you should make it clear that you aren't interested in dating other guys. Tell him you're okay with making that commitment, because I'll tell you right now that once Cooper falls, he won't even know any other woman exists."

"The questions is," Harlow chimed in. "Are you ready for Cooper and that kind of relationship? The Montgomery men can be a little… intense."

Taylor snorted. "That's putting it mildly. They love hard, Torie, and I don't think Cooper is an exception."

"He's not in love with me," I answered. "But I'm crazy about him. If he thinks I'm the one who isn't ready to take this relationship to another level, he's wrong."

"Then be bold," Harlow suggested. "I think he's going to be cautious because of your history if you don't."

"I'm…okay. None of us can heal overnight from a kidnapping, right? Dr. Romero is helping me. I think it's just going to take time. There are still some things that I haven't managed to get over."

Harlow nodded. "I still struggle with some things, but it gets easier every day. Your situation was a little different, Torie. Taylor and I were deprived, but we didn't have to go through the same physical recuperation that you did. Your injuries were pretty intense. I doubt you were really able to think about your emotional wellbeing for months."

I nodded. "I was in and out of surgery and physical therapy for months. I think because my physical injuries had to take priority, my mental health went on the back burner. I didn't have anything left in the tank to deal with that for a long time."

"You'll deal with your issues one by one as they pop up," Harlow said. "They won't all go away overnight, but putting them out there instead of burying them helps a lot. You know I'm always there for you if you want to talk, Torie. I might not have all the answers, but I'm always there to listen."

"Me, too," Taylor said adamantly.

I blinked back the spontaneous tears that welled up in my eyes.

These women were so damn willing to treat me like a cherished friend, even though they didn't know me very well.

"I'm here for you guys, too," I told them. "Thank you."

"No thanks necessary," Harlow said sincerely. "Taylor and I had each other, which made things easier once I got my head on straight. You went through your ordeal all alone."

"My brothers are supportive, but it's not always easy for me to talk to them about this. It's hard for them to hear about what happened. They feel guilty, even though they have no reason to feel that way," I explained.

"Neither one of us has siblings," Harlow said. "But every woman needs another woman to talk to sometimes. We understand each other." She paused before she added, "It looks as though you have another male admirer."

I smiled at her as I rubbed the belly of Jax's golden retriever, Tango. "He's such a sweet boy."

Harlow stroked Molly, Jax's adorable Lhasa Apso as she answered, "Both of these monsters are sweet when they want to be. Molly here helped with my nightmares a lot. Maybe you should take her home with you for a while."

I shook my head. "No way. She'd be crying for you and Jax, and my nightmares aren't really that bad anymore. I do find it amazing that she can actually sense your nightmares, though."

"She's a pretty amazing girl," Harlow agreed.

"The center and the whole program is wonderful," I told her. "I think I'd be in trouble if I visited there more often. I think I'd get extremely attached. I'm not sure how Cooper has managed to stay dogless."

Harlow rolled her eyes. "He's not. He just says that he is. That man is attached to every single dog at the center. He's just never singled one of them out. He usually spends more time there than Jax does, and he takes as many canines as he can manage out running as often as he can."

"So, they're essentially all his dogs," I considered out loud. "He just keeps them all at the same place."

"Exactly," Harlow answered emphatically. "You probably haven't seen it yet, but Cooper practically goes into mourning when one of the trained dogs goes to a new owner. Don't let him tell you he doesn't get attached."

I smiled as I kept stroking Tango's silky fur, not at all surprised by what Harlow had just revealed.

Cooper might be the quiet one, but the man's emotions obviously ran a lot deeper than he wanted anyone to believe.

Chapter 20

Cooper

"Was it really necessary for you to go back to sleeping at your condo?" I asked Torie as I watched her play with one of the puppies at the training center the following Friday.

I'd just finished taking several dogs for a run while Torie had taken a group of unruly puppies out for a walk.

We'd followed this same routine for the last several days, ever since Torie had decided that her dreams were under control enough for her to sleep alone.

She met me here in the evenings, dressed casually in a pair of jeans and a T-shirt.

We exercised the dogs.

And…she eventually went home.

Yeah. Okay. We generally ate first, but the bottom line was that Torie wasn't sleeping in my bed anymore, and I hated it.

When she turned her head and smiled at me, I could almost forgive her for abandoning me. "We always knew that arrangement was temporary, Cooper. I'm sure you're probably happy that I'm not using you as my personal electric blanket anymore."

I wasn't. "I never minded," I said unhappily.

Hell, if she really wanted to sleep in her own bed, who was I to stop her?

Truthfully, she looked happier. Probably not because she was sleeping in her own bed, but because she was slowly gaining confidence again and getting her sleep.

"Will Milo really have to go back to the shelter?" Torie asked in a woeful voice. "He's still a puppy."

The two of us were currently seated on the carpeted floor in the play area of the center, all of the trainers already gone for the evening.

Torie still looked beautiful, and smelled even better, even though she'd been working with the puppies for hours now. All I could say for myself was that I desperately needed a shower after a long run.

I shook my head. "I don't know. We'll try to find him a home, but he's an obedience school dropout. He's wicked smart, and he follows commands, but he can be a goofball, which is something we don't need in a dog that has to be steady for veterans."

She turned that beautiful pair of soulful amber eyes toward me as she said, "He's still a baby."

"That baby is about to become an adolescent. Yes, he's still a puppy, but he may never be steady enough to be a working dog," I told her.

Hell, I hated sending any animal to a shelter if I didn't have to, but almost every single one of my friends already had a dropout from my program.

I watched as Milo jumped up and started to lick Torie's face.

"Milo!" I said sternly. "Down. You know better."

I swore the canine shot me a dirty look before he responded and hit the ground right next to Torie's legs.

"See how good he minds," she said hopefully as she stroked her hand over his coat.

Fuck! It killed me to disappoint her, but Milo wasn't going back into the program. He was just too high risk for failing at his age.

The mutt was perfectly capable of doing the job.

He just wasn't always sure that he felt like doing it.

None of us were exactly sure of his dubious parentage. He had floppy beagle ears, a tan Labrador coloring, and his face was reminiscent of an Australian shepherd.

Yeah, he was cute, but he was a handful.

"He doesn't have the temperament for the program, Torie, but I'll see what I can do," I grumbled.

Her face lit up like a Christmas tree, and I felt my heart squeeze inside my chest.

She leaned toward me and wrapped her arms around my neck. "Thank you, Cooper. He's such a sweet dog. I don't want him to go back to the shelter, even if it is a no-kill shelter. Milo needs a home."

As she laid those soft lips over mine, I swore to God I'd find that damn mutt a home if it was the last thing I did.

Instinctively, I wrapped my arm around her waist and kissed her back, but I backed off the second we came up for air. "I probably stink," I warned her.

She gripped my T-shirt before I could go very far. "You smell delicious," she said in a sultry tone. "Like we just had hot, sweaty sex."

My eyes widened because that wasn't something that Torie would usually say. "It would probably be a lot sexier if that were actually true," I replied.

"A woman is allowed to fantasize," she said as she slowly let go of my shirt and got to her feet.

I practically stumbled to my feet and hefted Milo into my arms so I could put him back into his crate.

Fucking hell! What was this woman trying to do to me?

First she abandons me and my bed, and then she tells me she fantasizes about us having hot, sweaty sex?

I locked up after all the dogs were settled, and followed her to her vehicle. "What are you trying to say to me, Torie?" I asked her gruffly as I trapped her body between me and her car.

I wasn't going to let her get away until I had some answers.

I'd been fucking restless all week, and worried as hell that she wasn't ready to tackle her dreams all by herself yet.

Granted, she didn't have a nightmare all that often anymore, but what if she did?

Who in the hell was going to be there for her in the middle of the night?

Me!

Who in the hell was I kidding? If Torie had a bad dream, I'd be at her condo in record time.

Didn't matter if it happened at midnight or in the wee hours of the morning.

"I'm not exactly sure," she said as she wrapped her arms around my neck. "But I think I was flirting with you. I probably can't say it was seduction, exactly, but I'm working on that."

"Torie," I said in a warning voice next to her ear. "You just decided that you didn't want to sleep with me anymore. Please don't tell me you actually want to seduce me."

We were situated underneath one of the lights in the parking lot, so I could see her face clearly as she stared into my eyes and said earnestly, "I do. I am trying to seduce you. I'm just not all that practiced at doing the whole seduction thing. I'm back to sleeping at my condo because I'm ready to move on, Cooper. I don't need you to take care of me anymore like a friend or a casual date. I don't need you to be with me every night in case I have a bad dream. What I really want is a boyfriend who wants to take me to bed and fuck me until we can barely move the next day. When you're ready for that, let me know. Do you want to have dinner with me tonight?"

"You know damn well I want to have dinner with you *every* night."

She cocked her head as she shot me an innocent look. "Do I know that? Sometimes I don't think I actually know what you want, Cooper. You pull me forward, and then you push me away. What in the hell am I supposed to think about that?"

I had given her mixed signals at times. Hudson and Jax had been right. I'd confused Torie while I'd been trying to protect her.

"Is it really possible that you don't know what I want?" I asked her huskily as I palmed her cheek.

I saw her swallow hard before she nodded. "I'm tired of wondering, Cooper. I think I really need to know. I don't want to experiment anymore, and I know what I want. I. Just. Want. You. I don't want to date anyone else. I want an exclusive relationship where we spend as much time as possible together burning up the sheets. That's it. That's what I want. I won't promise you that I won't have some issues from what happened in the Amazon, but some of those things just need time to heal."

"Fuck! I thought you understood," I rasped.

"Apparently, I didn't," she answered. "You might need to explain that whole thing to me again."

"Clearer this time, obviously," I said tightly.

"I need you to at least understand one thing," Torie insisted.

"What?"

"I'm ready, Cooper. If you want the same things I do, I'm ready."

I tightened my arm around her waist. "I wanted you from the moment we met, but it was safer for me not to acknowledge those feelings at all. I want you to know that I hate myself for those first two weeks when we barely spoke. You were still recovering, and I could have been there to help you."

Torie stroked the hair at the nape of my neck as she replied, "No, Cooper. There's no way you could have known about my history, and you had no obligation to know. I don't want to go back there. I want to move on. With you, if you want me."

Christ! What in the hell had I ever done to deserve a real chance with a woman like Torie?

Whatever it was, I sure as hell wasn't going to spend another moment trying to screw things up.

Nor was I going to try to make sense of how badly I wanted and needed Torie Durand to be mine.

Those feelings were just…there. The emotions just existed. Whether they made sense…or not.

I wrapped my arms around Torie and claimed that gorgeous mouth because I couldn't wait another second to get closer to her.

When I finally released her lips, Torie murmured, "I have an early morning appointment tomorrow with Dr. Romero. It was the only time she could get me in this week. My place for lunch around noon?"

Christ! I wasn't sure I'd survive that long before we started this new relationship.

"I'll be there." Hell, I'd made it this long. Did another day really matter? "I want you to know that I've always wanted more than just casual dating. I'm not that guy who can have sex with you and walk away, Torie. It was never going to be that way for me."

I could feel her shake her head as she rested it on my shoulder. "I don't want it to be that way, either. I care way too much about you for it not to mean something to me."

Fucking hell!

I regretted every harsh word I'd ever said to my brothers about losing their minds because if Torie muttered one more revelation, gave me one more sign that she wanted to be with me, I was completely fucked.

Chapter 21

Torie

"Everything went fine, but this mission wasn't exactly smooth," Marshall, the leader of Last Hope, said from headquarters the next morning. "The local indigenous tribe got confused and thought we were the bad guys."

I didn't really need to be here at Last Hope headquarters this morning, but I wanted to be.

Apparently, a team had done an emergency rescue mission last night in the Amazon—which was right up my alley—so I'd decided to drop in when I'd gotten the usual text message that was sent to all Last Hope members when a mission was in progress.

Marshall was present, as well as Hudson, Jax, and Cooper. They all looked like they'd arrived long before Harlow and I had.

Harlow had hung around during the rescue, too, so she could monitor the weather conditions.

All of us were still sitting in the large mission room on the first floor of the headquarters trying to figure out how this group of river rats, also known as Amazon pirates, were operating.

I rose from my seat so I could examine the map up on the large screen. "I know this area," I told Marshall. "It's not far from where I was rescued. It has to be the same indigenous tribe that saved me. They aren't hostile, Marshall. I'm sure they were just trying to protect their territory."

The older man nodded. "I'm sure you're right. I just wish we could explain to them that there are pirates in their area, too, and we just needed to rescue an American citizen who shouldn't have been pulled off his boat to be a hostage. I'm not sure what's going on in that area of the Amazon Basin, but things have been heating up there lately. This new gang of river rats in that area are getting extremely active. Nothing new had happened since your kidnapping, Torie. And now, all of a sudden, there's been three pirate hits on small luxury cruises over the last month, plus this latest kidnapping."

I'd listened to the entire rescue from start to finish just in case anything was said that needed to be translated, and I'd been on the edge of my seat the entire time.

Marshall had sent in a team of four, and if the drama with the indigenous tribe hadn't come up, those guys would have been in and out of the pirate camp within minutes.

Honestly, the confusion with the tribe had nearly blown the mission.

I kept studying the map as I asked, "Do you think there could be more trouble with the pirates?"

Marshall shook his head. "I'm not sure, but judging by the activity, it's likely. This is the first time they've taken a captive, and the guys said he was unharmed, but boats are being hit for money and valuables, too. The pirates are so damn mobile that it's going to take a while to catch them. Hopefully, they're not as violent as the ones who took you hostage, Torie, but we only have a few incidents to judge by right now."

"Why now?" Cooper asked, sounding troubled. "Before Torie's kidnapping, nothing significant had happened in that area of the Peruvian Amazon in years."

I looked at Marshall to see if he was going to answer. When he didn't, I gave my opinion. "Sometimes these gangs of river rats move around like nomads. Once an area gets hot, they move to another. It sounds like they just moved in or back in recently. They'll stay for a while until things get too hot to risk anymore. Then they'll go somewhere else unless the authorities apprehend them first."

"Luckily," Hudson said. "Everyone got through this mission okay. I hope they stick to stealing and stop the hostage taking."

"It would make our life a lot easier," Jax agreed. "Especially since that indigenous tribe is so close."

"Maybe someone should talk to them," I considered.

"Do the tribes all speak Spanish?" Harlow asked curiously.

I shook my head. "The languages and dialects of the indigenous people are kind of complicated in the Amazon. Some of the tribes do speak Spanish, but many have their own language. The tribe that rescued me had members who spoke Spanish, but most communicated in their own dialect."

"Sounds confusing," Jax commented.

I smiled at him. "It can be, but you have to understand the history. There are still tribes there that have never come into contact with anyone other than their own tribe members, so they don't know anything about the world outside of their own tribe."

Hudson nodded. "I've heard about those no-contact tribes."

"They're pretty unique," I said. "Marshall, I could probably talk to the tribe. I know the leader, and I've always wanted to go back there to thank him for what they did. They saved my life."

"Over my dead body," Cooper growled. "That place nearly killed you."

I turned until I caught Cooper's gaze.

His eyes were fierce and unyielding.

"How could you work that out?" Hudson asked, ignoring Cooper's outburst.

I shrugged. "I would have to go there. Obviously, the area is remote, so there's no other way to contact them."

"Not. Happening," Cooper reiterated.

"Calm down, Coop. Let's get all the information first," Jax suggested.

I could tell that Cooper was in no mood to be reasonable.

Honestly, I'd never seen him act the way he was acting right now.

His expression was wild and unreadable, and I had no idea what he was thinking.

"She's not going," he rumbled. "Christ! We could never ask that of her. She nearly died there."

"But I wouldn't be going back under dangerous conditions," I explained. "I could get safe transport down the river until I got to the area—"

"Where there are now currently pirates," Cooper rasped as he slammed his hand down on the desk. "Be reasonable, Torie. It's not a no-risk trip. We know there are pirates in that area."

"We could keep her protected," Jax contemplated. "We could hire our own boat and send a bunch of guys with her as bodyguards."

Hudson shrugged. "We could make it fairly no-risk."

Marshall held up a hand. "This has to be totally Torie's choice. Would it help? Yeah, probably. We may have more incidents in that area and they're ransom cases the government isn't going to want to touch. But I don't want her doing anything that's going to make her uncomfortable."

"I speak enough of their tribal language to communicate well with them, and much of the tribe speaks Spanish, too," I explained to Marshall. "I spent a day in their village before I could get transport out of there, so I'm sure they'll remember me. If you want a representative to go and speak with them, I'd be your safest and least threatening person to do it."

Marshall shook his head. "Logically, yes, but are you up to going back there, Torie?"

"I don't think I'll know that until I get there," I said honestly. "The Amazon rainforest was once one of the locations I wanted to visit the most out of any other location in the world. Now, I'm not sure how I feel about it."

"It could trigger some really bad memories," Jax said carefully.

"He's right," Hudson agreed. "If you think it might set back your recovery from the kidnapping, it's not worth the risk, no matter how convenient it would be to have someone sort out the natives there."

"I think I could do it," I said.

Honestly, I wasn't certain how I'd feel about seeing the Amazon again, but I could manage if it could mean less danger for a future rescue.

"Are you certain?" Marshall asked solemnly.

I nodded. "I am."

"It's not fucking happening," Cooper said in a loud, graveled voice as he slammed his fist down on his desk again, but even harder this time. "It's too dangerous. It's risky to Torie's physical and mental health, and she's not setting foot in that goddamn jungle again. She left that place barely alive and with more injuries than most people could survive. We are not sending her back there."

Everyone in the room, including me, stared at Cooper.

I was assuming I wasn't the only person who had never seen him raise his voice like this.

"It's not your call to make, Coop," Hudson said calmly. "Torie makes her own decisions."

"What in the hell do you think Chase and Wyatt are going to say?" he rasped. "Do you think either one of them will be happy that we're suggesting that their little sister go back to the location that nearly killed her?"

"The Amazon didn't do it, Cooper," I said quietly. "Pirates nearly killed me."

"It's not Chase or Wyatt's decision, either," Marshall said.

"But they definitely won't be happy," Jax considered.

I took a deep breath and tried not to get too irritated. "My brothers never have and do not make decisions for me," I informed everyone. "I'll speak with both of them and let them know what I'm doing, but I don't need their permission to leave the country."

"I don't want you to go," Cooper said gruffly. "You're staying here."

I glared at him.

This hadn't been an easy decision for me, and it pissed me off that he was being such a jerk.

"I was hoping you'd support my decision, but apparently all that matters to you is getting exactly what you want," I told Cooper tersely. "I hate to break it to you, but you don't run my life, either, Cooper Montgomery. Oh, and by the way, that rational brain of yours doesn't seem to be functioning this morning. I thought we both agreed that trips to the Amazon are minimally risky and that I was just in the wrong place at the wrong time."

"That was before a new group of river rats moved in," he grumbled.

I didn't answer. What was the point?

If this was Cooper's idea of the way an exclusive relationship should be, then maybe I was better off passing on it.

Tears filled my eyes as I grabbed my purse and headed toward the exit as I said, "I think we should consider our lunch date canceled."

I was crazy about Cooper Montgomery.

I'd thought we were ready to start a new and much more intimate chapter of our relationship, but how was that even possible if he was going to act like a tyrant?

My heart wrenched as I left Last Hope headquarters with all of my hopes and dreams for my future relationship with Cooper Montgomery completely in shambles.

Chapter 22

Cooper

"I'll talk to her," Harlow said as she went to follow Torie. She paused before she left the room to look at Hudson and Jax. "I think you guys had better speak to the caveman dictator here before he screws up every chance he has with the best thing that's probably ever happened to him."

She didn't hesitate again as she left the building, and the entire operation room went dead silent once she was gone.

Marshall was the first one to speak. "Well, I'd better get upstairs to my office and get a report written up. I doubt you need me here."

The older man moved pretty damn quickly for a guy with an injury that had ended his military career.

He was gone seconds later.

I crossed my arms over my chest as I turned to face my two brothers. "Please don't tell me you would have handled that differently," I requested irritably.

Hudson shot me a dubious look. "Are you serious, Cooper? I've never seen someone handle a situation worse than you just did. Torie is a grown, intelligent woman. What made you think you could make a major decision for her like that?"

"Because I can't possibly watch her go back to a place that probably holds some of the worst memories of her entire life," I rasped, my emotions out of control. "I've been there with her when she wakes up in the middle of the night from a nightmare. How do you think I feel when I see the terror in her eyes? How would either one of you feel if Harlow and Taylor were planning on going back to Lania to help Last Hope?"

"I get it," Hudson answered. "I hate that fucking country, but I'll tell you one thing: Taylor wouldn't be going alone. Has it ever occurred to you that you could be with Torie on this journey instead of pushing her away by being a major dick?"

I pulled my head out of my panic and fury long enough to think about what Hudson had just said.

I could go with Torie.

I could be there to protect her.

This time, she didn't have to be in the Amazon alone and vulnerable.

"I guess I wasn't thinking," I confessed. "All I could think about was her going there alone."

I'd never really been a partner with any woman I'd dated.

They wanted things and money from me, not my emotional support.

Hell, I wasn't sure I even knew how to be that really supportive kind of boyfriend she needed, but it was something I really yearned to give Torie.

"She doesn't have to make this trip alone, Coop," Jax said. "Maybe she needs to go back. Sometimes one of the things that helps a victim is facing their fears by going back to the scene where everything happened. It helps them get some closure by recognizing that only the people who held them captive were evil. Not the place where it happened."

I looked from Jax to Hudson. "Do you think it would actually help her?"

"I don't know," Hudson admitted. "It might."

"Fuck!" I cursed. "All I want is to make her happy, but I think I just managed to screw everything up instead. Jesus! I'm not cut out for this. I think I lost it."

"Fix it or you're going to be miserable," Hudson advised. "I get why you had a knee-jerk reaction, but Torie obviously doesn't. She was hurt because you weren't hearing her, Coop."

"All I could think about was how she looks when she wakes up from one of her nightmares," I grumbled. "Christ! I haven't had a rational brain since the day I met Torie Durand. She makes me absolutely insane. All I want to do is protect her so nothing like that ever happens to her again."

Jax smirked. "I never thought I'd ever say this to you, Coop, but you really need to pull your shit together. Maybe you should just tell her how you feel."

"How am I supposed to explain that I'm completely unreasonable when it comes to her?"

"I think you'll have to explain why," Jax replied. "Tell her you're worried about something happening to her."

"Isn't that obvious?" I asked.

Hudson shook his head. "Not really. Torie was right. You did sound like you just wanted to get your way since you didn't exactly explain yourself."

"So now she thinks I'm a selfish prick?" I questioned.

"Possibly," Jax answered. "Just talk to her, Cooper. You can straighten this out, but you can't just tell her what you want without discussions and compromises. Torie is used to being independent. I'm not really a great one for advice on this topic since I push Harlow pretty hard sometimes when it comes to her safety, but she lets me know when I'm being an asshole by pushing back. It takes a while to learn how to compromise. I love her so damn much that I want to keep her safe at any price, but I have to manage to keep her safe and make sure I'm respecting what she wants at the same time."

Shit! I hadn't meant to disrespect Torie. At all.

Yet, I had by not talking to her before I insisted she wasn't going back to the Amazon.

I ran a frustrated hand through my hair. "Now what the hell am I supposed to do?" I grumbled.

"She looked pretty upset," Hudson mused. "A certain amount of groveling might be necessary."

"I'm not too proud to grovel," I told him. "Hell, I wasn't thinking about how my reactions sounded to her. I just wanted her to be safe."

"What happened to my younger brother who always thinks before he makes a final decision?" Jax asked.

"His brain leaves his head every time the woman he's crazy about walks into a damn room," I rumbled unhappily.

"She feels the same way, Cooper," Hudson said thoughtfully. "She wouldn't be hurt if she didn't."

I stood up and snatched my keys and my cell phone from my desk. "I'm going to have to find a way to get her to talk to me."

"Don't take no for an answer," Jax advised.

I nodded. "I don't plan on it. I'm just trying to decide my plan of attack."

Probably the best way to start was to send her a text and see if she'd answer.

ME: *I'm sorry...again. Can we talk?*

Not that I actually planned on waiting for her to respond. More than likely, she wouldn't.

I hadn't been the one who had canceled our lunch date.

She canceled.

I hadn't agreed, right?

"What exactly does a guy bring to a groveling session?" I asked my brothers, wanting all the advice I could get.

Failure was not an option.

"Sincerity and emotions are recommended," Hudson counseled.

"Heartfelt gifts are completely optional," Jax finished.

"Shit!" I cursed nervously. "I have absolutely no clue how to turn a woman's head or make her forgive me for doing something stupid.

I'd give anything to have just a small amount of your charm, Jax. I've never been good at talking to women that way."

Jax shook his head. "You don't need it, man. Just give Torie your heart."

"She has it," I confessed hoarsely. "Probably has since the day we met."

Hudson slapped me on the back. "Everything will work out fine. Harlow will calm Torie down."

I shot my brothers a skeptical glance. "She didn't sound too happy with me, either."

"Nah. She adores you," Jax argued. "She's just not crazy about the dogmatic way some guys like to try to resolve issues sometimes. She thinks I'm a tyrant when I'm trying to protect her, and I've started to recognize that she's probably right. But sometimes I can't stop that initial reflexive reaction."

"Taylor feels the same way," Hudson griped.

"And I just did the very thing that independent women hate?" I asked, knowing it was a rhetorical question.

"Guaranteed, it won't be the only time it happens," Hudson warned. "You're always going to want to know she's safe, and she's always going to want her complete independence. Those two things will clash occasionally. Just remember that what you want isn't always necessarily right for her. Learn to compromise."

"I'm not crazy about the idea of her going back to the Amazon," I confided. "But if I'm with her, I'll deal with whatever happens. I may need to take some time off."

Hudson shrugged. "It's not like you didn't cover for us when we needed it. Jax and I aren't going anywhere."

Jax grinned. "I'm way too happy to even think about changing anything up. Do what you need to do. Montgomery Mining will be here when you get back."

I swallowed hard. No matter how much the three of us might disagree and give each other a hard time, I couldn't wish for better brothers to have at my back when I really needed them. "Thanks. I'll call you later and let you know how things go."

I strode across the room and toward the exit.

"If we don't hear from you, we'll assume things are going well," Jax called after me in a joking tone.

One way or another, I was going to figure out exactly how to fix *everything* I'd screwed up between Torie and me.

I'd never see my rational brain again if I didn't.

Chapter 23

Torie

COOPER: *I'm sorry…again. Can we talk?*

I sighed as I looked at Cooper's text for the umpteenth time in the last several minutes.

I sat at my small kitchen table chewing on my thumbnail, willing myself not to answer, but it was getting more difficult by the second.

Harlow had stopped by my condo for coffee, and she'd managed to convince me that Cooper wasn't going to become a tyrant the moment we entered an exclusive relationship.

Honestly, I'd already known that. I knew Cooper well enough to recognize that his behavior earlier wasn't typical.

I'd just been hurt because he'd blown off every word I'd said and surprised because I'd never seen him that intense.

Now that Harlow was gone, I was having a difficult time stopping myself from answering Cooper's text.

I wanted to talk to him.

I wanted to know what he was thinking.

And I wanted to make it clear that I had a mind of my own that I'd been utilizing for thirty-two years all by myself—thank you very much!

I sighed and dropped the phone onto the table.

Maybe my biggest problem was that I had no idea what to do with a guy like Cooper. My past relationships had been lukewarm at best, and usually ended the same way. I'd had boyfriends, but they'd never really touched my life the way Cooper had.

I'd never spent every single day with any of those guys.

They'd never been there to take care of me if I was injured or sick.

I'd never been giddy with anticipation and excitement to see them again.

Sadly, not a single one of the guys in my life prior to Cooper had ever made my female hormones get up and dance, either.

I was no innocent virgin, but Cooper Montgomery made me feel the kind of desire I never knew existed.

I was so deep in thought that I startled when the doorbell rang.

Deep breath, Torie. It's probably not him.

"Torie!" Cooper's voice bellowed in the hallway as he knocked on the door. "I know you're home. I saw your car in the parking garage. Open the door."

I rose from my chair, my heart racing as I moved closer to the front door.

Obviously, he wasn't patiently waiting for me to answer his text. I had no idea why his impatience took my breath away.

He knocked louder. "Open the door, sweetheart. We need to talk."

I melted. His tone was slightly desperate but determined.

Stepping up to the door, I slid the chain off and flipped the deadbolt before I pulled the door open. "I do have neighbors, Cooper," I admonished with very little censure in my voice.

As he stepped in and closed and locked the door behind him, I released a breath I hadn't realized I'd been holding.

He was in the same jeans and ice-blue Henley shirt he'd been wearing earlier. The one that almost matched his beautiful eyes.

I turned and walked into the kitchen with Cooper following on my heels.

"Before we say another word, I need to tell you a few things I should have said a long time ago," he said huskily as he wrapped his arms around me from behind, finally catching up to me as I reached the sink. "Okay?"

I nodded, closed my eyes and leaned back against him until my back was plastered against his front. I was helpless when he was holding me like this.

I could feel his heat, his passion flooding from his body and into mine.

"Did you know that I'm so damn crazy about you that every time I see you I can hardly breathe?" He rasped the question right beside my ear.

I shook my head.

"Well, I am, goddammit! I don't think rationally anymore when you're around, and I do really stupid things. Hell, I've never been a guy who believed in fate, but I think I knew I was fucked from the moment we met. There was something there. Something that couldn't be defined by logic. It was nothing tangible and nothing that made sense, and I sure as hell shouldn't have known almost instantly that you were supposed to be mine. But that's exactly how I felt."

My heart was hammering against my chest wall as I turned until I faced him and wrapped my arms around his neck. "I felt something, too. I knew you were different from every guy I'd ever known."

The frost in his gaze melted as he looked down at me like he wanted to devour me whole.

His expression was fierce, but his intensity didn't scare me. Instead, I wanted to move into that heat until I was on fire.

Cooper tightened his arms around my body. "I acted like an asshole today because just the thought of anything happening to you scares the hell out of me, Torie. I never want to see you afraid again, and I think I'd probably kill any man who ever raised a hand to hurt you. Christ! All I want is to see you happy and not haunted by what happened to you in the Amazon. I lost it when I thought about you having to go back there."

Tears started to pour from my eyes unchecked as I raised my hands to his head and stroked his hair, trying to soothe him somehow. "I don't have to go back, Cooper. No one is forcing me. I think it's something I have to do to completely heal. My trauma was all intertwined with a place that I always imagined would be almost magical. I think it's time for me to separate the two of them while I help Last Hope at the same time."

"Fine," he grunted. "But I'm going with you, and I'll be fucking armed to the teeth. I'll arrange our own transport with people I trust to keep you safe. You okay with that?"

I beamed at him. No matter how grumpy he might sound about the whole idea, I had to admit that taking an armed and dangerous Cooper Montgomery with me didn't sound like a bad idea at all. "I think I could live with that."

"There's nothing I won't do to keep you safe, Torie," he warned.

"Thank you," I answered simply.

He leaned his forehead against mine. "For what?"

"For caring that much about me. I shouldn't have left like that from headquarters today. I guess I just felt like an idiot because you weren't listening to anything I said," I explained.

He stroked a hand up and down my back. "I'd never want to make you feel that way, baby. Fuck knows, it couldn't be further from the truth. I'll listen next time. I can't promise you that I won't screw up in this relationship again if you give me another shot, but no one could be sorrier than I am right now because I made you feel anything less than fucking perfect."

My heart somersaulted inside my chest as I saw the earnest expression on his face and the genuine remorse in his eyes.

I stroked my palm over his whiskered jaw. "We'll both make mistakes. I think that's probably what happens when emotions run hot between two people."

"My emotions aren't the only thing that runs hot when you're around," he said, right before his mouth came down on mine.

My heart sang and my spirit soared as our lips said everything our vocal chords hadn't already said.

His kiss was demanding, sensual, and covetous.

By the time I came up for air, I was literally panting.

"Say you'll be mine, sweetheart," Cooper said in a panty-melting baritone as he traced my bottom lip with his thumb.

I wasn't sure if there was actually any question in his command, but I gave him what he wanted. "I think I probably always have been," I answered as I fell into his possessive gaze.

"So, exclusive relationship back on?" he asked as he raised a brow.

Shit! Like I could really resist a man like Cooper Montgomery? I nodded.

"When are we leaving for the Amazon?" he questioned.

I took a deep breath. "Whenever you're ready, but I think I'm going to need a little help with one final thing before we go."

Chapter 24

Cooper

Of all of the things Torie could have asked from me, the only thing she'd wanted was to come over and use my indoor pool. Not that I'd minded getting her half naked, but I could see the fear in her eyes as she entered the pool room in a modest one-piece black swimsuit.

I watched from my place in the middle of the pool as she slowly approached the water.

She sat and dipped her feet in at the shallow end. "This pool is enormous," she said in a nervous tone.

Fuck! Something wasn't right.

My gut was sending me the same warning it had when I talked to my brothers about the fact that I still sensed something was wrong with Torie.

I swam over to where she was dipping her toes, stood between her legs and wrapped my arms around her body as I said, "Tell me."

It wasn't like I didn't know that something had happened to make her wary of getting into the water. I'd just been waiting for her to tell me exactly what that issue might be.

She put her hands on my shoulders in a completely trusting manner that tore my guts apart before she said, "Whenever I put my head underwater, I panic. It's one of those remaining issues that I just can't seem to shake. My kidnappers liked to play this twisted game whenever we were in the boat. They'd grab my hair and shove my head under the water until I thought that I was going to die. Before they did it, they even told me that they were going to kill me. I believed them, so I fought back with everything I had, but it was never enough against the strength of two monsters holding my head under the water."

"Fuck! And then they pulled you up before they drowned you?" I said, trying not to let my voice betray my fury. I had to remember that this was about her, not me.

It was just really hard to remember that when I'd just found out one more way Torie had been subjected to horrible psychological torture.

She nodded. "I think I passed out briefly once or twice, and I swallowed enough river water to make me pretty sick. It's been that one messed up thing that I haven't been able to conquer. Just getting into the water makes me nervous, and dunking my head starts the flashbacks. I haven't tried getting into the water for a while because of it. But I love the water. I don't want to let those bastards win."

Jesus Christ! What kind of twisted fuck did something like that?

Every muscle in my body went taut with the need to kill those two bastards, but I tried to shake it off as I asked, "Are you ready to try again. I'll be right here, Torie. Nothing will happen to you. I promise."

"Yeah," she answered anxiously. "I think I'll be okay. You make me less afraid."

I tightened my arms around her and slowly wrapped her legs around my waist. "We'll do this together."

I watched her chew on her bottom lip as I walked us slightly away from the side of the pool.

I stopped and held my breath as she slowly lowered her legs down to the cement at the bottom of the pool. We were in the shallow end, and once she was completely down, her head was still well above the water.

"Okay?" I asked huskily as I held her head against my shoulder, wanting to protect her.

"I am okay," she said, her voice slightly stronger. "The water feels amazing."

I wasn't about to tell her that I cranked up the temperature as soon as we'd gotten to my place, so the cooler water I usually preferred wasn't a shock to her system.

She raised her head and slowly released her death grip around my neck. "Now for the final challenge," she said as she stepped away completely and took a deep breath.

She lowered herself under the water, but came up sputtering and gasping for breath. "Shit!" she spat out as she swiped the water from her face.

I took her hand and hauled her against me. "You're okay, sweetheart."

Her eyes were slightly wild as she said, "I know, dammit! It's not quite as bad as it used to be, but I just can't seem to forget—"

"Kiss me," I demanded. "Wrap yourself around me and we'll go down together."

I had no idea if having a distraction would help, but it couldn't hurt.

She sent me a sultry smile that made my damn cock ache as she questioned, "Are you offering yourself up as a very beguiling diversion?"

"Hell, yes. If it helps," I growled.

Torie wrapped her arms around my shoulders loosely and speared her fingers into my hair. "When your lips are on mine," she purred. "I can never think of anything but pleasure."

Yeah, well, that might not be true since she'd been severely traumatized, but I was ready to try anything that might help her. Torie loved the water too much. She had to get over this hump.

She fused her mouth to mine, and I let her lead the way as we both sunk underneath the water.

I could sense a brief moment of panic before she capitulated and continued that cock hardening kiss until we had to surface to breathe.

"Holy shit!" she panted. "Distraction works."

We "practiced" over and over until Torie finally took my hand and shot under the water on her own.

"It's better," she said excitedly as she came to the surface. "Maybe I just needed something pleasant to balance the horrible memories."

I knew she wasn't completely cured, but as I watched her dive under the water over and over again as she repeatedly swam the length of the pool, I knew she was going to be okay.

Torie had once been completely at home in the water, and she'd feel that way again. She just needed time to let go of the old stuff.

"Have I told you what a completely amazing guy you are tonight?" she asked after she'd swum back to me and thrown herself into my arms.

She wrapped her legs around me, and I happily palmed her ass to keep her close.

Nah. She hadn't told me that, but I sure as hell wasn't complaining. Torie was here, and she was exactly where she belonged. That was more than enough. "Ready to get out?" I asked. "I'll hit the shower and call for some dinner."

She nipped at my earlobe before she whispered, "Are you starving?"

"Not really. Do you want to go out?"

"No," she said emphatically. "I was going to suggest that you take me with you into the shower and I'll fix us something to eat…later."

Fucking hell! That was the best idea I'd heard in…well…pretty much forever.

"After the misunderstanding today, are you sure?" I asked. "Fuck! I need you to trust me, Torie, and I screwed that up today."

"No," she said with a shake of her head. "You didn't. I trust you, Cooper. I know those words were coming from a place of fear, and I know it won't happen again because you know that you hurt me."

My gut twisted as she said those words. "Are you sure you're ready for this?"

She swiped the hair out of her face as she said, "I'm tired of misunderstandings and waiting, Cooper. All I really want is to be with you. Everything else will work itself out, but I can't stop this horrible ache inside me that just won't go away."

She ached.

I wanted to soothe any discomfort she had.

Basically, it had been this way since the very beginning.

It would be a fucking relief to finally give her exactly what she needed.

If I couldn't fix every issue she had left over from her kidnapping, I could at least take care of the need that radiated between the two of us.

I lifted her up and climbed the steps until we were out of the water. "I'm not even going to ask if you're certain one more time because you've had plenty of chances to run away," I muttered as I carried her into the house.

"I don't want to run away," she assured me as she trailed kisses up my jawline. "I want you to fuck me, Cooper."

Christ! There was no way she was getting away from me tonight. Just hearing those words from her gorgeous lips made me half crazy.

"Be careful what you wish for," I warned as I sprinted up the stairs and to the master bathroom. "It could end up being more than you want."

She lowered her feet to the floor as I turned on the rain shower that ran with multiple jets.

"I'll never get enough of you, Cooper," she purred into my ear. "Never. All I want right now is to touch you. That's all I've wanted since the first time I saw you."

I dropped my trunks to the floor as Torie skimmed the lightweight suit from her body.

I took her hand and pressed it against my rock-hard cock. "This is what you fucking do to me, Torie. What you've always done to me."

I held my breath because it was the most intimate thing we'd ever done.

She was naked.

I was naked.

Her hand was finally on my cock.

And she still wasn't running.

Hell, she didn't even look the slightest bit nervous.

She pulled me into the shower eagerly and reached for the nearest shampoo and body wash. "Just let me touch you, Cooper. You don't have to move. You don't have to do anything. I just want to get to know this gorgeous body of yours."

I closed my eyes as Torie began to run her hands all over my body, smearing my hair and skin with body wash as I grunted, "I'm not sure how long I can handle this right now, sweetheart."

Fuck! I wanted her to touch me, but not reacting to the best damn sensations I'd ever felt was going to be next to impossible.

She'd definitely break me and my patience.

"You're so beautifully made, Cooper," Torie cooed as her hands stroked down my back to fondle my ass.

"Torie," I said in a voice meant to make her use some caution.

"Don't ask me to stop," she pleaded. "Not yet."

I dunked my shampooed hair under the water to rinse it as I gritted my teeth. I didn't ever want to deny Torie something she wanted...

"Fuck!" I cursed loudly as Torie wrapped her fingers around my cock and dropped to her knees.

Jesus! She wasn't really planning on...

She wouldn't...

"Christ!" I cursed when her mouth connected with my cock.

I was a big guy, and there had been very few women in my past who had even wanted to attempt to wrap their lips around me.

I fucked, and for the most part, that had been enough.

Until. Right. Fucking. Now.

I buried my hands into her wet hair and fisted the locks. She swirled her tongue around the tip before she swallowed as much of the shaft as she could handle.

"Jesus," I growled. "You're killing me, woman."

"Are you complaining?" she asked between licks up and down my cock.

"Hell, no," I groaned.

However, if she didn't stop using my cock as her personal lollipop, I couldn't be responsible for the consequences.

It felt too damn good.

She felt too damn good.

This kind of intimacy felt too damn good.

"Enough," I growled as I pulled her to her feet.

As good as it had felt to have my cock in that beautiful mouth of hers, I needed a few other things much more.

"You didn't like that?" Torie asked as she looked up at me.

Christ! Did she really have to ask that question?

Had no man ever told her that she was a sexual goddess and the fulfillment of every single one of his fantasies?

"Everything you do is right and fucking fantastic," I assured her. "But that's not the way things need to end right now."

Hell, no.

I needed to be inside her.

I needed her body completely locked around mine.

I needed to hear her screaming my name in pleasure as she climaxed.

Nothing else was going to satisfy me or her this time.

Chapter 25

Torie

I shuddered as Cooper's hands stroked sensually over my skin. He was returning the favor of lathering up my body and hair with a body wash that smelled like vanilla and another scent I couldn't quite place.

Honestly, my brain wasn't working and most likely wouldn't as long as Cooper was touching me like this.

He rinsed my hair and then my body before he captured my mouth with his and devoured it like it belonged to him.

I fisted his hair and kiss him back, starving for the intimacy we hadn't completely found…yet.

"Oh, God, Cooper," I panted as he let go of my lips, tugged my head back with my hair, and proceeded to feast on the skin at my neck. "I need you. Please."

"You're so fucking beautiful, Torie," he growled against my skin as one of his hands wandered between my thighs.

"Yes," I hissed as Cooper teased a finger over my clit.

"You'll get my tongue later," he promised in a graveled voice right beside my ear.

"Is that a threat?" I said breathlessly. "Because I'm actually looking forward to it."

"It's a goddamn promise," he answered hoarsely right before he nipped my earlobe. "Do you have any idea how long I've waited to touch you like this, Torie. It feels like forever, and this is the embodiment of my every fantasy right now."

My head thumped against the shower enclosure as I closed my eyes and let myself drown in pleasure.

Cooper knew exactly how to make a woman crazy with his fingers and his mouth.

I whimpered as the pressure of his finger stroking my clit increased and he sped up his pace. "Cooper!"

"Tell me what you want, Torie," he demanded.

"I need you to fuck me," I moaned. "I ache, Cooper. I ache."

I needed to get closer to him. I wanted to crawl inside him and never come out again.

"I'll never be able to let you go after this," he said.

Like that was a bad thing? I didn't want him to let me go now or ever.

"I'll never let you go, either," I said like it was a vow.

"I'm clean, Torie. Birth control?" he asked harshly.

"I have an IUD that's been in for a couple of years. I'm covered, Cooper. I'm clean. You don't need a condom."

"Thank fuck!" he rasped as he pushed me against the wall of the shower. "Hold on to me."

I wrapped my arms around his neck and put my legs around his waist as he gripped my ass.

"You okay?" he asked as our eyes locked.

I knew what he was asking. "I'm not thinking about them, Cooper. I couldn't. Not when I'm with you. What they did was torture. That wasn't like this. It could never be like this. This and you are everything."

"Only pleasure here, sweetheart," he answered right before he covered my mouth with his.

With one surge of his hips, Cooper buried himself to the hilt inside me.

I gasped against his lips because he was a large man, and he stretched me until it was nearly painful.

He raised his head and looked down at me, concerned.

"Okay, baby?" he asked as he suddenly stopped, his large hands still squeezing the cheeks of my ass.

Cooper crowded me, he surrounded me, and his concern radiated through his voice until it was nearly palpable. "You're so big," I moaned. "Just give me a second."

"I'll give you forever, Torie," he promised in a husky tone right next to my ear.

I shivered from that lusty promise.

"I'm better," I said a short time later as I rocked my hips against him. "Fuck me, Cooper."

Pleasure rushed in as he pulled back and then surged back into me again.

And then, my body cried out for satisfaction.

I no longer ached.

I craved.

I coveted.

I hungered for Cooper Montgomery in a way I never had before.

"Christ! You're tight, Torie. You feel so damn good," Cooper groaned as he started pumping into me faster and faster.

Tears filled my eyes as my emotions started to overwhelm me. "I've wanted this. I've wanted you for so long."

"Hey," he said coarsely. "Don't cry, baby. What's wrong?"

"Happy," I told him. "Don't stop. Please don't stop."

I threaded my hands through his wet hair, trying to absorb every bit of carnal pleasure I could get.

"Harder," I urged Cooper, needing to be as close to him as I could get.

He gave me what I wanted, and I started to moan his name over and over as my body tightened. "Cooper. Yes. That feels so good."

"You're mine, Torie," he said fiercely. "Say it."

"Yes!" I screamed. "Yes, I'm yours."

Cooper started a breakneck pace and shifted slightly so each time he buried himself inside me, it would stimulate my clit.

God, I'd been so close when he'd first buried himself inside me that I could already feel my climax hurtling toward me.

"More," I pleaded, my body begging for release.

Cooper gave me more as he grunted, "Come for me, sweetheart."

"Oh, my God. Cooper," I whimpered, my body no longer my own.

I buried my nails into Cooper's back and lowered my forehead to his shoulder as my orgasm pounded over me.

"Fuck, yeah," he rasped. "Let go, baby."

I did, knowing that he'd catch me if I fell.

"Fuck!" he groaned as he grasped my hair and tipped my face up so he could watch me lose it. "You look so fucking beautiful when you come."

I felt his muscular body shudder as the spasms of my climax milked him to his own release.

I panted as I sagged against him, trying desperately to catch my breath.

"I think that orgasm just killed me," I complained breathlessly.

Cooper squeezed my ass. "You feel perfectly fine to me."

I swatted his shoulder. "I nearly died and I'm not sure you even worked up a good sweat."

He chuckled against my shoulder. "Sweetheart, with that sexy fuck-me voice of yours urging me on, there's no way I'm not going to be sweaty. Did that help all of your aches go away?"

I smiled against his shoulder. "For now. But I'm sure they'll come back again later."

"Then stay with me," he requested huskily. "I'd be more than happy to take care of every one of them for as long as they keep popping back up."

God, I knew *that* would be an eternity.

I was never going to stop wanting this man.

I was never going to stop needing him.

There was never going to come a time that I didn't want to be with him.

Cooper was my elusive Mr. Right.

I wasn't sure if I was alarmed or elated.

While he was quite expertly pleasuring my body, I'd also realized that he managed to steal my heart, too.

I was completely, irrevocably, terrifyingly in love with Cooper Montgomery.

"You went quiet. Everything okay?" he asked as he stroked a gentle hand over my wet hair.

I'd always known my emotions were out of control when it came to Cooper, so maybe it shouldn't have surprised me all that much that I was in love with him. "Just taking a rest," I said lightly.

I was not going to let the way I felt about him scare me away from the best thing that ever happened to me.

Yeah, it was scary, especially when I had no idea if he loved me back. But if I'd learned nothing else during my kidnapping, I'd discovered that nothing was guaranteed.

I was going to hang on to Cooper and enjoy the ride for however long it lasted.

When I'd been afraid that I was going to die in the Amazon, my one big regret was the fact that I'd never had an intense love affair in my life.

Cooper could give me that…and more.

Once I'd stopped rolling in post coital bliss, I slowly lowered my feet to the floor of the shower.

I wallowed in the pleasure of Cooper washing me all over again, and I took my time returning the favor.

By the time he finally shut off the water, my fingers were completely pruned and my body was still trembling.

I watched, drooling as I finally got the chance to ogle his powerful, naked body as he quickly dried himself off.

Cooper *was* every woman's fantasy. From his muscular biceps to his six-pack abs, his nude body was a work of art.

He quickly tossed his towel and brought a fluffy one to dry my body off.

I reveled in the intimacy of something so simple as Cooper taking his time to dry every inch of my exposed, damp skin.

By the time he was done, I wanted him all over again.

"Food?" he asked as his hungry eyes roamed over my body. "I did promise to feed you."

"All I really want is you," I said honestly. "Unless you're starving, feel free to just take me to bed, Cooper."

I felt like I'd waited so long to be with him like this that I had more exploring to do.

"Food is really highly overrated," he replied hoarsely as he lifted me into his arms and headed for the master bedroom.

Chapter 26

Cooper

"I can't claim that I kidnapped you, but I did finally get you into this incredible jet for an adventure," Torie teased as we lounged on the wide couch in the cabin of my private jet on our way to Peru.

Hudson had sent his jet to Michigan to pick up some of our guys who operated together in the same city there. They'd be our backup, our security, and I was grateful they'd all volunteered to help me out. We'd all be rendezvousing in Iquitos for the trip down the river.

I wasn't taking any chances.

I'd bought out a riverboat that usually did river cruises to carry us into the jungle. The captain and the small crew had all been hired and approved by Marshall, which meant they had some kind of ties to Last Hope.

I'd turned down Hudson and Jax's offers to accompany us since I had plenty of guys meeting us on the boat, and someone had to stay behind to run Montgomery. The last time all three of us had left at the same time, Taylor and Harlow had been kidnapped in Lania.

Torie had explained what her plans were to Chase and Wyatt, and although they weren't thrilled about her return to the Amazon, they were okay with the way we were doing the traveling.

Both of her brothers had offered to fly back to come with her, but she'd blown them off since they weren't ready to leave Paris.

And me? Hell, I was the happiest bastard that ever existed just because I'd spent the last week knowing that Torie was mine.

That she had no desire to see anyone except me.

Thank fuck!

I'd even decided to adopt Milo myself because Torie loved the mutt so much, and her reaction had been more than worth the effort of getting the pup comfortable at my place.

I wrapped my arm around her and pulled her on top of me. "Are you sure you're going to be okay? It's okay to be nervous, you know."

She smiled at me, and my heart kicked against my chest wall.

That was all it took.

One smile.

One look.

One kiss.

And Torie Durand could knock me on my ass.

She stroked her fingers over my jaw and I closed my eyes because each gesture of affection she gave me was so damn sweet.

"I really won't know how I'm feeling until I'm actually there," she explained. "But I've watched countless videos of the area over the last week, and it's not making me cancel the trip."

"Videos and reality are different, sweetheart." I didn't want to burst her bubble, but she was bound to have some kind of visceral reaction at first.

The sounds.

The smells.

The water.

None of it was all that real in videos.

One look of true fear in her eyes and I swore that I was throwing her ass over my shoulder and getting back on my jet.

It was a big world, and there was no damn reason she had to visit that small part of it ever again.

She sighed. "I'm not going to deny that I'm a little anxious. I think the sights and sounds will all come back to me as soon as we get there. I might need you to hold my hand for a while, but I think I'll be okay."

I grinned at her. "I'm completely available for whatever needs you might have, hand-holding included."

She lifted a brow. "Are you?"

"Absolutely."

"When it comes to you, I'm always pretty needy," she murmured close to my ear.

And I'm always there and eager to take care of those needs.

Christ! After the last week, I would have thought the poor woman would be sore and totally exhausted.

I could barely keep my hands off her long enough for her to get a decent night's sleep.

Our seemingly insatiable appetite for each other was incredible for my ego, though.

It was obvious how much she wanted me, which made me feel like the biggest stud in existence.

"I think I might be ready to accept that job at the university," she said. "The more I've dug into the job description, the more interesting it gets. I might have to teach some classes occasionally, but even that would be kind of fun."

"Will you be happy?" I asked. As far as I was concerned, that was really all that mattered.

"I think I will," she said. "Obviously I won't know until I try it, but I think teaching languages and cultures is pretty important."

"Then I think you should give it a shot. If it's not your thing, there are plenty of other jobs out there for a woman with your skills and talent. Are you hungry?" I asked. It had been hours since we'd boarded in San Diego, and we hadn't eaten a thing yet. "The kitchen area is well stocked with food so you don't have to cook."

She nodded. "Maybe after that, we can play a game of chess."

I shot a glance at the large chess table I had set up in the corner. "Not happening."

She frowned. "Why not? I do play. I doubt I can give you a huge challenge but it might be fun, right?"

"Can't," I said. "I'm pretty much unbeatable, and I don't like to see you unhappy. Therefore, I'd hate beating you all the time because you'd always lose."

I wasn't trying to be a prick. I was just stating facts. I didn't want to demolish her at chess and then get her naked. There was something wrong with that whole scenario.

She shot me one of her are-you-serious-right-now looks. "That's completely twisted. You play with your brothers and I know you've played with Taylor."

"That's different," I said uncomfortably. "I'm not in an intimate relationship or fucking any of them."

She raised a brow. "Have you ever played with a girlfriend?"

"Hell, no. I've never had one who even knew the basics of chess."

"Did it ever occur to you that I could learn to be a pretty good player if we played over and over again? You could teach me to beat Chase and Wyatt," she said. "I'm actually not a sore loser. If I was, I never would have suggested it."

Hell, I'd never thought about that. That idea was slightly appealing. "Have you ever beat either one of them? They're both really good."

"No," she answered with a disgruntled expression. "I can give them a challenge occasionally, but I've never won a game."

I was pretty sure Chase never let Torie forget it, either. Maybe it would be entertaining to watch Torie kick that crap out of him.

"I'll think about it if you really want to play," I told her. "When I'm alone with you, the last thing I think about is a chess game."

"I think we could definitely find something else interesting to do," she agreed with a sexy smile.

I rolled her over on her back and stared down at her gorgeous face.

Fuck! I was so used to seeing that smile every damn day. I was getting so used to Torie accepting me, even if I wasn't exactly normal.

Or romantic.

Or charming.

She got me like no one else ever had, and that shit was completely addicting.

"Do you ever think that we spend an abnormal amount of time together?" I asked her without thinking about my words.

She looked a little confused. "No. It's never felt like that to me, but if you're sick of seeing—"

"Fuck! No, sweetheart. That's not what I meant. I've always been… separate from anyone I dated. Our lives weren't….intertwined. At all. It's not *our* relationship that's strange. I think my past relationships were odd."

"How so?" she asked.

I explained how things had always worked for me while she listened carefully.

"So you planned your weekly outings, but you never did anything else together? Did you even talk on the phone or text in between dates?" she asked.

"Not unless we had a problem with our date night," I confessed.

"I'm sorry, Cooper. I'm so sorry that not a single woman you dated ever really saw you because you're someone incredibly special," she said earnestly.

And just like that, Torie could completely disarm me with a compliment like that, just because she thought I was someone special.

"None of them matter as long as you think so," I said as I leaned down to kiss her.

Little by little, Torie was teaching me what it really felt like to have someone care about me and not everything I could give them.

And it felt…amazing.

Was it really any wonder that I never wanted to lose her?

"I do think so," she murmured. "I think you're the most incredible man I've ever met and sometimes I have to pinch myself to remind myself that you're real. Especially when you saw my crazy eyes in the dark and you didn't run away screaming."

I nuzzled her ear as I said, "Hottest thing I've ever seen."

Torie's eyes were extraordinary, and on the rare occasion when the low light was just right, they did glow in the dark. And it *was* one of the sexiest things I'd ever seen because she was almost always in a state of sexual arousal at the time.

"There's definitely something wrong with you," she joked. "But you won't hear me complain because you think everything about me is sexy."

"You're beautiful, Torie, and there's not a single thing about you I would change, even if I could," I said honestly as I started to unbutton her shirt.

"You make me feel beautiful," she answered breathlessly. "Over and over again."

"I'm going to take the time to appreciate all of that gorgeousness this time," I warned her.

Every time I touched her, I swore we were going to take it slow, but once that torch caught fire, there was no way to stop the inferno.

"One of these times, we'll actually manage to take it slower," she said breathlessly as she reached for my shirt. "But I have a feeling it won't be this time."

Turned out, she was absolutely right.

Chapter 27

Torie

I woke in the dead of night in pain, and completely confused. It took me a minute to process the fact that someone had a hard grip on my hair braid and a gun to my head as they yanked me into a sitting position.

The light was dim in our tent, but one of the pirates had a flashlight, so I could see what was happening.

Cooper had his Glock trained on the pirate that had a handgun at my skull, and his gaze on the one who didn't that was standing right beside me.

The men were all in a standoff, and none of them looked like they were ready to move.

"Don't do anything stupid," the male voice holding the gun said harshly in Spanish. "You're coming with us."

I looked at Cooper, who didn't look like he was ready to back down.

In fact, his expression was murderous.

Dammit! Everything had gone so well over the last few days.

Even though I'd been apprehensive at first, I'd relaxed pretty quickly once I'd gotten on the riverboat in Iquitos and realized how many people were there to protect my ass.

Our trip down the river had been uneventful and our hike into the jungle to reach the indigenous tribe had taken most of the day, but the results had been everything we'd hoped they would be.

I was reunited with the fisherman who had saved my life, and I'd been able to deliver all my gifts of thanks to the tribe.

We'd also been able to explain about Last Hope, the situation with the pirates, and the possibility of future kidnappings. The tribe had been cooperative and had promised not to interfere in the future if members of Last Hope needed to enact another rescue in their area. We'd even figured out a special item of clothing Last Hope volunteers could wear so the tribe could identify them.

The native people had invited us to dinner in their little village and had taken Cooper and the two men who had hiked in with us to a site where they could pitch their tents for the night.

Since it would be a day hike the following day to get back to our riverboat, Cooper had gratefully accepted.

I suddenly squeaked as the pirate holding my braid yanked on it harder.

What the hell? Had the indigenous people betrayed us?

I immediately discarded that thought. The tribe had absolutely no reason to do that. More than likely, the river rats had seen us hiking on our way to the village.

"I don't think they can speak or understand English or they would have given us orders we could understand," Cooper said, his voice coarse. "I could probably get two shots off and kill them both before they could shoot, but I can't take that risk, Torie. He could very well pull the trigger even if I shot him first."

I listened as the pirates exchanged words, both of them speculating about what Cooper was saying.

"They don't understand you," I told Cooper. "They also don't know why we're here, but it sounds like they think we're investigating the kidnapping of their last victim that Last Hope rescued. The tribe knows nothing about this. The pirates have been watching us since they saw us hiking in earlier today."

Cooper and I were silent as the two men talked, but Cooper didn't move a muscle. Maybe he wasn't going to be able to shoot because the pirate had a gun to my head, but he wasn't backing down his stance at this point, either.

I finally asked, "Do you think I should scream to try to wake up the others?"

The two men who had come with us were in tents not that far away.

"No," Cooper said sharply. "They both look pretty nervous. It could startle them or they could shoot just to shut you up. I don't want them pulling that trigger."

"They didn't expect you to have a weapon. They don't know what to do," I translated to Cooper.

"Fuck!" Cooper cursed. "I have zero room to maneuver in this tent. I can't take the two of them down without the risk of that gun going off."

"They're talking about two more guys outside, so there's four of them here," I told Cooper. "The two outside are keeping watch on the other two tents in case one of our guys wakes up."

The pirates became more agitated because they couldn't understand what Cooper was saying.

They didn't like him talking when they couldn't decipher what he was planning.

"Put the gun down," the pirate with the gun spat out at Cooper in Spanish as he tapped the barrel of his weapon against my head.

"They're losing it," Cooper rasped as he slowly put the gun down on the top of the blanket. "Whatever happens, stay calm, sweetheart. If they wanted us dead, they would have already tried to shoot."

"It sounds like they want a hostage to take the place of the one who was rescued. I don't think this group is highly organized or sophisticated. I think they're a new group and not affiliated with some of the others that are more established. They're just desperate for money," I relayed.

The pirate without the gun reached out and retrieved the one Cooper had just given up. He lifted it toward Cooper and my heart sank.

Stay calm, Torie. Stay calm.

A heated discussion ensued between the river rats as they tried to figure out a plan.

Did they want to take both of us?

Did they want to just take me and leave Cooper behind?

They decided that wouldn't work because Cooper would probably come after them immediately.

Did they want to slit Cooper's throat with the knife in their pocket and just take me because I'd be easy to handle?

After that suggestion, I couldn't stay silent. "You'd be an idiot to do that," I told them in Spanish. "He's an official in a high position with the United States government. If you kill him, they'll find you and they'll either kill you on the spot or make sure you never leave prison."

There was a momentary silence, probably because the pirates were surprised, but then they started peppering me with questions.

Did Cooper have money?

Did his family have money?

Who was my family?

I finally held up a hand as I said, "He has power, but no money. I'm a very rich woman with very little power. Take me. You'll get paid to let me go, and leaving him behind will ensure that they won't send a powerful army after you."

After listening to the two of them talk, I'd realized they weren't particularly worldly. I was pretty sure they'd believe my lies.

I squeaked again as they dragged me to my feet by my hair.

Luckily, Cooper and I had bedded down fully clothed.

"You better not be lying to us," one of the men grunted.

"I'm not," I assured him.

"Torie," Cooper growled. "What in the hell are you saying? What are they saying? What in the hell is going on? You need to clue me in here."

My heart stopped as one of the pirates walked up beside Cooper and slammed him in the head with the butt of his pistol until Cooper lost consciousness.

"I told you not to hurt him?" I said angrily.

"He's not dead," the pirate behind me said as he moved the gun from my head and jabbed it into my ribs. "Move."

The tent went dark as the second river rat with the flashlight moved out of the tent.

I quickly pulled my necklace off under the cover of darkness and tossed it toward Cooper without my captor seeing the action before I moved out of the tent.

Cooper would have no idea what I'd said or what had happened.

He wouldn't know if I was dead or alive, but I was hopeful the lack of blood would tell a story.

God, please let him just wake up with a little headache.

The bastard had slammed Cooper in the head pretty hard.

How injured would he be when he woke up?

After the two other men joined us, the group started to march me through the jungle.

Without much thought, I covertly reached into the pocket of my jeans and pulled out a handful of tiny beads that I'd been using to make necklaces with the women in the village.

I dropped one, and since they only had one flashlight that the lead pirate was holding, no one noticed.

As we continued to move, my imagination went wild, and I was thrown back to another time when I was held captive because some things were familiar.

The gun shoved into my ribs.

The sound of two men trying to formulate a plan as we trudged through the jungle.

The feel of rain on my skin.

The heat of the rainforest when the humidity was close to a hundred percent.

A few tears escaped from my eyes, but I suddenly shook off my sense of gloom and doom.

That was another time, a different circumstance.

This time, I wasn't without hope.

I wasn't alone.

I had every bit of faith that I was going to be rescued.

If Cooper was capable of rescuing me, he would.

If not, my brothers would turn this rainforest upside down until they found me.

All I had to do was keep my head on straight.

I dropped another bead.

And then another after we'd walked for another few minutes.

How far did we have to go?

How long would we be walking?

I had no idea, but I kept my brain in a place of calmness and hope as we continued on.

Chapter 28

Cooper

"Miller and Davis are following the beads that Torie tossed out, and Marshall says he'll have a location by this afternoon. You've got to calm the fuck down, Cooper. Miller says he's sure you have a concussion and that you're bleeding like a pig," Jax told me as we talked on the satellite phone the next morning.

"I can't calm down and I don't give a shit if I'm bleeding. They took her, Jax. I couldn't protect her. They ambushed us in the dead of night," I said, my voice hoarse with emotion.

I was still sitting in the same spot my ass had landed on near our tent after I'd spent more than an hour covering the general area looking for Torie.

It had taken us a while to find the beads because they were so tiny, but I'd immediately recognized them as the ones Torie had been using earlier for necklaces.

Miller and Davis had insisted on following the beads once we'd located the first one since I was bleeding everywhere and I was having double vision.

I was no fucking help to them at all.

Since I hadn't been able to see straight, literally, I'd agreed to contact Marshall and start working on some of the other mission details.

I'd needed to do…something.

I'd called Jax soon after.

"We'll get her back, Coop. But you know you have to wait until it's dark and you have an exact location. Hang in there, brother. We're taking her back tonight."

I raked a hand through my hair, oblivious to the blood that was soaking my shirt and my hair. "What if they hurt her before we can execute a goddamn rescue…"

I couldn't even deal with the possibility of something even worse happening.

"We will rescue her and they won't hurt her. She's no good to them injured or dead. You said you didn't see any blood coming from anywhere except your own body," Jax answered. "Are you sure you're even able to head this mission?"

"Are you really asking me that question?" I barked. "What if it was Harlow? If you were conscious, would you be sitting on the sidelines?"

"Dumb question," Jax answered flatly. "You're right. But I also know you're injured."

"I got hit on the head. I'm not dying," I answered gruffly. "Christ! I don't even know why that happened. I think it was something that Torie said to them. She was definitely trying to convince them to do something."

"Do you think she was trying to talk them into taking just her?"

"I'm almost sure of it," I answered. "She left the necklace I gave her and she did it on purpose. It wasn't broken. She slipped it over her head."

"Why?" Jax asked, sounding confused.

I explained the necklace to Jax and why I'd given it to Torie before I said, "Her leaving it behind was a message. She's saying to come get her, that she knows I'll rescue her. That I'll free the oppressed, who just so happens to be her right now. Fuck! How can she still have that much faith in me when I couldn't even protect her when we were together? I had that bastard's head in my gun sight—"

"Stop!" Jax said sternly. "No one could have done anything different from what you did, Cooper. You had to give up the gun or risk Torie getting shot. There's absolutely no question about that. Now we just need to focus on getting her back."

My heart was hammering in my chest as I told him, "Oh, she's coming back. Tonight. I'm not leaving her in their hands one second longer than I have to."

"Just remember that your mission is to get her out of there. I know you're pissed, Coop. I would be, too. But keep it covert. Get in and out as quickly as possible and get back to the riverboat. Leave the justice to the Peruvian authorities. We'll make damn sure they show up after you get Torie out of there. Marshall wanted to get a helicopter to you, but the vegetation is too thick."

"Doesn't matter," I answered. "The beads are headed toward the river. I have a feeling we won't have to go far to get back to our boat. It makes sense that they're camped near the river."

"He is sending a helicopter to the riverboat to bring you both back to Iquitos for medical treatment," Jax informed me. "You were out for a long time, Coop. The bastards probably cracked your skull."

I had one hell of a headache, and my vision still wasn't quite normal, but my adrenaline was so high that I hardly noticed my head injury. "I'm fine. But send it in case Torie needs medical attention."

Jax let out an exasperated breath. "You can't help her if you're not healthy."

"Do you really think I give a fuck right now?" I asked Jax huskily. "After all she's been through, how could I have let this happen?"

"You didn't," Jax snapped. "You had no way of knowing those bastards were following you. They have to be newbies because it makes absolutely no sense for them to approach you anywhere near that village. Just focus, Cooper. It doesn't matter what happened last night. Keep your eye on today. You've got Miller and Davis with you, and they're a few of the best. Even if Torie didn't have enough beads, Miller can track them. The beads will just make his job easier.

You three can have Torie out of there in a matter of minutes. That's all that matters right now."

"Fuck! You're right," I told him grimly. "I can deal with this other shit after I have her back."

"You want me to call Chase and Wyatt?"

"They deserve to know, even if there's nothing they can do right now," I answered harshly.

"I'll call them," Jax replied. "Let Miller clean up those gashes on your head so you don't scare the shit out of Torie."

"I have to get her back, Jax," I said gutturally. "What in the hell was she thinking when she tried to get them to leave me behind?"

"I'd say she was trying to protect you, just like you'd do for her if you could have spoken the language."

"Why?" I asked, my tone desperate.

"I'd think that was pretty damn obvious," Jax said drily.

"Christ! Doesn't she know that I love her, that I'd die before I'd see anyone lay a hand on her ever again?"

"Maybe you've never told her, but I kind of think she already knows that, Coop," Jax answered. "I think she also knows that you'll be there to rescue her. She's pretty much telling you that by leaving the beads and her necklace."

"She has to be fucking terrified after what happened to her a year ago," I told Jax.

"These aren't the same guys," Jax replied. "Those bastards enjoyed hurting her. She's not going to be coming back to you like that, Coop. She won't even be with these pirates for twenty-four hours."

"She told me that she didn't think this group was very well-organized, so I think you're right about them being newbies," I explained to Jax. "She was listening to their conversation. They didn't understand a word of English."

"There isn't exactly a high entry bar to being a river rat," Jax said thoughtfully. "Just a group of some desperate men and a few weapons. She obviously didn't think they were connected to other organized groups."

"She didn't think so," I answered flatly. "There were four total near or in the tents last night. I don't know if there are more or if that's the whole group. It really doesn't matter because we'll get Torie back one way or another."

I sure as fuck wasn't leaving that pirate camp without her.

It didn't matter how many assholes called the place home.

"You got enough firepower?" Jax asked.

"We came prepared for trouble even though we weren't expecting it. Unfortunately, Miller and Davis had everything in their tents since mine was sleeping two. I think that's why they ambushed our tent. They were watching us and I think they assumed I didn't have any of the weapons."

"They got your Glock, right?" Jax asked.

"Yeah, but it doesn't matter. We have better weapons and plenty of ammo."

"You haven't done an op for a while," he reminded me.

"I'm not going to fail," I vowed somberly.

"Didn't think you would," he said. "I wish I was there right now, Coop. Hudson feels the same way. I wish I could be at your back."

"You will be. At headquarters. I'll be counting on you, Hudson, and Marshall pretty heavily. I'm not exactly familiar with the Amazon Rainforest. We can use as much intel as we can possibly get."

I'd need all of them for guidance and coordinates.

"We're already at the headquarters. Harlow is on the weather," Jax informed me. "You're at the very beginning of the really rainy season in the rainforest. She said the heavy rains can be ruthless. We'll keep you informed."

I didn't answer because Miller and Davis were jogging toward me.

"We found the camp," Davis said as he abruptly stopped in front of me.

"Where?" I asked.

"We've got some hiking to do," Miller said. "It's back toward the river. Your Torie did a hell of a job leaving those breadcrumbs. We could have tracked her, but she made it a lot less complicated. Those beads were definitive proof that we were staying on the right track.

She must be something to have thought about dropping those beads when she was being kidnapped."

I nodded. "She is something."

Hell, she was everything.

Miller and Davis wandered away to start getting some equipment together.

"They found the camp?" Jax asked.

"Yeah. Tell Marshall we got our coordinates. This mission is playing out as soon as it's dark."

I wasn't going to wait a second longer than was necessary. We needed the cover of darkness, but I wasn't leaving Torie with those bastards one moment longer than it took for us to get in there and rescue her.

"Stay safe," Jax said gruffly. "Bring everyone back in one piece, including yourself."

"I don't give a shit what happens to me as long as Torie comes back safe," I grumbled.

"I care," Jax rumbled. "Hudson cares. And God knows Riley cares. Get your ass back here unharmed."

"I'll do my best," I told him, my mind still focused on Torie.

"Try to cut yourself a break, too. This wasn't your fault, Coop. Focus on what you have to do and remember that. I would have reacted exactly the same way. I wouldn't have chanced Harlow getting shot at point-blank range," Jax said firmly.

My head started to spin as I stood up, but I ignored it. "I'm going to find Miller and Davis so we can get this mission worked out between the three of us here."

If I didn't start doing something, I was going to lose my mind.

Jax and I disconnected with the promise to check in again once we were on our way to our rescue location.

Hopefully, we'd be on our way soon.

I'd much rather wait somewhere closer to Torie, even if I had to wait for darkness to fall.

Chapter 29

Torie

I was jolted awake for a second time in the Amazon Rainforest, but my awakening was much gentler than the first time.

"Torie, I'm getting you the fuck out of here!"

Even though I couldn't quite open my eyes, a smile formed on my lips.

Cooper.

It wasn't like I hadn't known he'd come, but I was glad he'd finally arrived.

"I knew you'd come," I said, my words more than a little bit slurred.

I felt him lift me into his arms, and moments later, I could feel the rain on my skin as he started to move through the jungle.

"I'll light your way and Davis will watch your six," Miller said in a quiet voice.

"Let's move as quickly as possible," Cooper requested. "Something's not right with Torie. I need to get her to the boat."

Not right with Torie?

I tried to process that statement and initially failed.

Once I thought about it again, I said, "I'm okay, Cooper."

"No, you're not all right," he answered in a harsh whisper. "There's blood on your face and I could hardly wake you up, sweetheart. What the fuck did they do to you?"

He sounded frantic, so I forced myself to concentrate. "I'm not really hurt. I think I'm drugged. My face is bloody because I fell. I really am okay, Cooper. I swear. Are you? Oh, my God. How is your head?"

"The least of my worries," he grumbled.

"Where are we? I lost direction after a while last night, but I knew you'd find me."

"It's a hike back to the boat," he answered. "But we should make it there in a few hours."

"You can't carry me for two hours," I protested. "God, I hate this. I feel so damn helpless. I think the pirates wanted to sleep, so they decided to make sure I was so dopey that I couldn't go anywhere. Let me try to walk."

"Nope. I'm your ride right now, baby. We need to make time. You're going to need to get medical treatment," he replied. "I want to make sure you're okay."

I blinked, trying to get my eyes open for more than a second.

My brain felt like it was filled with cotton as I tried to get my bearings. "It's just the drugs. They didn't hurt me, Cooper. I'm more worried about you. They hit you really hard."

I might be slow, but I could remember everything that had happened.

"Maybe if you hadn't convinced them to leave me, they wouldn't have hit me," he said sharply.

"They weren't going to take you, Cooper. They were going to slit your throat so you'd die silently. I couldn't let that happen," I said tearfully. "I'm so sorry. I didn't know they'd hit you like that, but I couldn't let them kill you. I convinced them that you were someone important in the government, and that killing you would bring the U.S. government down on their head. I told them I was wealthy and I'd be an easy hostage to get money from because my family would pay a ransom."

I started to sob because every fear I'd had was suddenly clear.

"So you saved my fucking life by offering up your own," Cooper said hoarsely.

"Not really," I said glumly. "I knew you'd come to save me if you could."

"That's a lot of faith to put into a guy who couldn't save you when we were together," he rasped.

"Don't be silly," I insisted. "You had no other choice but to give up your weapon, even though I knew it killed you to do it."

"I was supposed to be in this damn rainforest with you to protect you, Torie," he said in a guttural tone.

"And here you are," I said, my voice still slightly off. "You put together a team and you're here to protect me. You're my hero, Cooper."

"Not the same thing as keeping you out of danger in the first place," he argued.

"Of course it is," I disagreed. "I've never had a man come to my rescue before. It's kind of…romantic."

Cooper released an exasperated breath. "I think you're still stoned."

"I think you're wonderful," I shot back at him. "You're my knight in shining armor, Cooper Montgomery."

"I doubt your brothers will think so," he said drily.

I tried to make out his face, but it was much too dark. "I thought my opinion would be more important than theirs," I huffed.

I heard him chuckle. "It is, sweetheart. Do you have any idea what they gave you? You sound pretty high."

"No idea," I informed him. "They didn't tell me they were drugging me or I wouldn't have drunk the water or eaten the food."

"So you started feeling off right after you ate?" he asked.

"Whatever they gave me, it was pretty strong. I almost went face first into my fruit. How long was I out?"

"What time did you eat?" he asked.

I thought for a minute. "Later in the afternoon."

"So, maybe a few hours," Cooper guessed. "We came in not long after sunset. Are you sure they treated you okay? Your makeshift hut had some ventilation and your bindings weren't cutting off your circulation, thank fuck."

"I didn't exactly do a lot of chatting with my captors, but they didn't mistreat me, Cooper, and they didn't touch me, if that's what you're worried about. They just…drugged me," I shared.

"No offense, sweetheart, but that fact is pretty obvious," he said, his voice a little lighter than it had been before.

"My brain is mushed," I said unhappily.

"We'll get it fixed," he promised.

"Actually, I don't mind so much," I told him happily. "It's probably similar to being really, really drunk. Not that I'd know what that's like. I've never drank enough at one time to find out."

"I have," he said grimly. "It's not so bad when you're under the influence, but it truly sucks the next day."

"The hangover?"

"Yeah."

I considered his words for a moment. "I don't think I'd like that."

"I guarantee you wouldn't."

"So how long are you planning on carrying me around?" I asked. "You've already done this once. Although it was probably easier in the park than it is for you in the rainforest."

"I don't give a shit how long I have to carry you," Cooper grumbled. "I'm just damn glad I have you in my arms alive and well."

"It just doesn't really seem fair that you always have to carry me around. I can walk, you know."

He snorted. "Not right now you can't. Baby, you'd land flat on your face. And I know you're perfectly capable of walking. Just let me carry you right now."

"I don't think I have any choice," I considered. "Are you sure you're okay? I can't see you. It's too dark."

"Now that you're with me, I'm fine," he said hoarsely. "Jesus Christ, Torie. You scared the shit out of me. I hope you've seen enough of the Amazon Rainforest because I really hate this fucking place."

I sighed. "I'm not all that crazy about it myself, but I really would have liked to see the pink dolphins."

"We'll see how we feel in five or ten years," he grunted. "Let me get over this trip first."

"Okay," I answered agreeably. "You sound tired, Cooper. Are you sure you don't want me to walk?"

"I probably sound older," he answered. "I think you took about ten or twenty years off my life."

"I was worried about you, too," I confessed. "I was more worried about you than I was about me. At least people knew where I was this time. They knew I was in the rainforest."

"That didn't mean that the bastards couldn't hurt you between the time they took you and your rescue."

"I suppose not, but the actual kidnapping would have been over quickly."

I snuggled into Cooper's muscular body and rested my head on his shoulder, relieved that he was obviously okay.

At some point, I fell asleep again, and I didn't wake until Cooper called my name.

"Torie? Sweetheart? We're back at the boat."

My head felt much clearer this time, and I was oriented almost immediately. I wasn't sure how long I was out, but it had been enough time for the drugs to start wearing off.

I could see the lights of the riverboat in the distance.

"God, Cooper, you have to be exhausted."

"Glad we're here," he said, his words slightly uneven.

"Cooper? Are you okay?" I said, feeling slightly panicked because he sounded stressed. "Put me down."

He ignored me and didn't stop until we strode over the dock and onto the riverboat.

I wriggled until he finally set me down on my feet.

I gasped the second I could finally see his face.

Blood was still trickling down from his head to his face, and the shirt he was wearing was saturated with blood.

The areas of his face that weren't covered with blood were so ghostly white that it terrified me.

"We made it," he said as his big body swayed.

"Dear God, Cooper! What happened?" I asked, my voice slightly hysterical.

He looked at Miller and Davis. "Make sure she stays safe," he said tersely.

"You got it, man," Miller said. "Let me help you get to your room."

He never got close enough to Cooper to help him.

I heard myself screaming in fear as I reached for Cooper.

In the end, I couldn't hold him up as his eyes rolled back in his head and he collapsed to the floor.

Chapter 30

Cooper

"Talk to me, Torie," I pleaded with her as we started our return trip from Iquitos to San Diego. "You've been taking care of me for four days now, but we've barely exchanged a personal word during that time."

After I'd collapsed on the riverboat, I'd gotten transported to Iquitos for medical treatment.

I'd suffered a skull fracture and a severe concussion, but after they'd fixed up the large gashes on my head, most of my treatment had been observation only to make sure I wouldn't have any other issues.

I didn't, so we'd boarded my jet today for our return trip to San Diego.

We were now leveled off, and it looked like we were going to have a smooth flight for now.

"What would you like to talk about?" she asked politely as she sat down at the other end of the couch from me.

"How about why you're so damn distant," I suggested.

I couldn't complain about her attentiveness or the way she'd taken care of me after I'd gone into the hospital.

Problem was, she'd never gone back to the old Torie, who was relaxed and happy when we were together.

"Maybe because you're so damn stubborn," she replied. "You didn't have to endanger your life that way, Cooper. God, you shouldn't have even been on your feet, much less carrying me for hours. You had a skull fracture. A skull fracture, Cooper. That's serious. That's not something to mess around with. And the amount of blood you lost was insane. Were you trying to kill yourself?"

I lifted a brow as I looked at her.

I wasn't angry.

Hell, how could I be when every word she said was because she'd been worried about me.

"If I remember right, I think you risked your life for mine," I reminded her. "I'd say what you did was more dangerous than me rescuing you and carrying you back to our boat."

"That's different," she said unhappily.

"Why?"

"I did what I did because I love you, dammit!" she said tearfully. "Did you really think I could sit there and watch them kill you? It would kill me, too."

I was temporarily stunned. "You…love me?"

"Yes. How many times do I have to say it? I'm crazy about you, Cooper Montgomery. Madly, insanely, absolutely in love with you. So it kills me to know every step you took on that rescue mission was pure agony and life endangering for you. You could have let Davis and Miller carry me out of there. Hell, you could have let them run the entire mission while you got medical treatment. Are you completely insane?"

I couldn't stop the grin that slowly started to form on my lips.

She thought I was insane?

"But it was perfectly okay for you to talk those pirates into taking you and not slitting my throat because…why?" I said, asking for clarification.

"Because I knew I'd get rescued," she said testily. "But it really wasn't necessary for you to do that yourself."

I was grinning like an idiot by the time she'd finished speaking. Hell, I was still floating on a cloud because she'd told me that she loved me.

"Did it ever occur to you that I rescued you for the very same reason?" I asked her, still incredulous. "I love you, too, Torie Durand. I was absolutely terrified when I realized the pirates had taken you and not me. I didn't know if they'd hurt you before I could rescue you. I didn't know if you'd be okay. Do you have any fucking idea how torturous that day was for me? Christ, you nearly died in that goddamn rainforest and knowing I'd failed to keep you safe there the second time around nearly killed me. Do you really think I'd let anyone do a rescue that critical to me? There's no other person that had so much at stake because there will never be a man who loves you as much as I do."

I moved closer to her, wrapped my arm around her waist, and pulled her into my lap.

"There is no me without you anymore, Torie. If something happened to you I'd never survive it. So that's why I had to make sure you got back to the boat safely. Do. You. Understand?"

Eyes wide, she looked at me and slowly nodded her head as she said, "I didn't know you loved me, too."

"How could you not know, sweetheart?" I asked her gently. "I think I've been pretty damn obvious."

"But you've always been the one to put on the brakes when things moved too fast," she murmured.

"Torie, you were kidnapped and brutalized until you nearly died a year ago. What kind of asshole rushes things after something like that. I didn't want to screw anything up. I told you I suck at romance and imagination. I had no idea how to charm you into being interested in me. But I was crazy about you from day one. So I told myself to be patient until you were truly ready for a relationship and then I'd have to hope that you'd give me a real shot. I told you that I knew from the beginning that you could never be just a fuck for me. I needed everything or nothing."

A tear plopped onto her cheek as she said, "Cooper Montgomery, I don't know who ever told you that you were unromantic, but she was wrong. Not all women want to hear bullshit that isn't true. I feel beautiful, desirable, smart, and special whenever I'm with you. And maybe some men can toss out the words, but what guy carries a woman for hours when he's critically injured himself? What guy offers to be friends because he knows that's all a woman can handle right then? What guy takes care of a woman every day for a week when she's injured? What guy sleeps with a woman every night just to try to make her nightmares go away? What guy adopts a puppy just to make a woman happy? What guy celebrates a woman's birthday when it's not her birthday? God, Cooper. Do you really not realize that the things you do *are* romantic? You just have the wrong definition of romance."

I shook my head. "Any guy would do those things—"

"No," she said as she put a finger to my lips. "No, they wouldn't. I'm here to tell you that no man does things like that except you. If another man like you exists, I've certainly never met him."

"You don't need another guy like me because you have the original," I grumbled. "Do all those things really make you happy?"

She nodded. "Yes. *You* make me happy, Cooper. Knowing you love me makes me absolutely ecstatic."

"I'm pretty elated that you love me, too," I told her as I threaded my hands into her loose, silky hair. "I'm going to be a pain-in-the-ass protective lover," I warned her. "Probably a jealous one, too."

She leaned over and gently kissed the top of my head. "I can handle that, Cooper, as long as you talk to me. And you'll never have any reason to be jealous because I don't see any man but you."

"I don't think the Montgomery men actually need a reason to be jealous," I considered. "Possessiveness seems to come natural to us the moment we fall in love. Maybe because we have it so good that we're terrified that happiness will be taken away."

Maybe I should have been concerned that I'd turned into a happy lunatic, just like my brothers, but I didn't give a damn. As long as Torie was mine for the rest of our lives, I didn't care how crazy I sounded.

"I'm not going anywhere, Cooper," she cooed against my ear.

"Then marry me, Torie," I said impulsively.

"Cooper?" she said softly.

Okay, so that proposal had sucked. "I'm sorry. I'll propose again and try to make it more romantic. You deserve the most romantic proposal I can possibly make, and you definitely deserve to have a ring on your finger when I ask. But I want you to understand where this is going for me, Torie. I want you to be my wife."

"Yes," she said firmly. "That's what I want, too."

My heart kicked against my chest wall. "I'll find you an amazing ring, and I'll set up something more romantic."

"I don't want another proposal. You asked once and I accepted. You're committed, mister," she teased. "But I will take the ring when it's ready."

Hell, I'd find her the most amazing ring out there.

"It could be awhile before we can actually get married," she said. "Harlow and Jax just got engaged, so we have two other weddings first."

"Oh, hell no," I told her. "I'm not waiting for my chance that damn long."

"There's always Vegas," she said.

"You'd want to do that?" I asked.

"I wouldn't mind at all," Torie answered. "I've never thought the wedding was as important as the honeymoon. And I will be hijacking you for a honeymoon."

"Where are you taking me?" I asked curiously.

Hell, not that I really cared. I'd go wherever she wanted to go.

"Let me think about that. It's going to have to be special," she replied as she put her fingers gently through my hair. "God, Cooper. These wounds still look bad."

"They don't really hurt anymore," I told her. "But they shaved enough spots to do the repair of those lacerations that I'm sure it's not pretty."

I didn't have a whole lot of hair at the moment.

"You look incredibly handsome," she corrected as she stroked my jaw.

Our eyes locked, and I grinned at her. "If that's true, then show me."

"Cooper Montgomery, you just got out of the hospital," she admonished.

I pulled her head down so my lips were so close to hers that I could feel her warm breath against my mouth. "I've missed you."

"I've missed you, too," she said breathlessly.

Torie squealed as I lifted her off the couch and headed for the bedroom.

"Cooper, you're still recovering," she protested weakly.

"I'm completely recovered and there's only one thing I need right now to make me feel better," I told her with a grin as I let her put her feet down next to the enormous bed.

She shook her head as she grabbed the bottom of her shirt and lifted it over her head. "I know I should be arguing, but I can't," she said wistfully. "I want you too damn much."

I yanked my T-shirt over my head. "I need you, Torie. I have to convince myself that you're fine, and that you're mine."

We tore at each other's clothes until we were both naked.

I gently pushed her onto the bed and came down on top of her knowing I was going to do everything I could to make sure she knew exactly how much I loved her.

Chapter 31

Torie

"You're barely out of the hospital, Cooper. What are you doing?" I moaned.

Tears filled my eyes as I remembered just how easily he'd told me that he loved me back.

And to think that he didn't believe he was a romantic?

Didn't he know that real love didn't depend on flowery, fake words or practiced seduction?

"I'm about to hear the most beautiful sound I've ever heard," he said huskily as he kissed and licked his way from my knees to my thighs.

Once he arrived exactly where he wanted to be, he spread my legs wider and slid his tongue up the inside of my thigh.

"Oh, God. Stop. Just make love to me, Cooper. We could try to go slow this time. You still have stitches in your head, for God's sake."

I really didn't want to stop him, but I'd already been through hell wondering if he was going to be all right after he'd gotten his head beaten in.

I reached down for him, but he pinned my hands to my side as he buried his head between my thighs.

"Oh, God," I groaned as Cooper's tongue licked my pussy from bottom to top, and then stopped to play with my clit. "Cooper!"

"Still want me to stop," he said in a teasing voice.

"You should…I shouldn't want…"

"Baby, I'm here to give you everything you want," he said huskily right before he sucked the swollen bundle of nerves into his mouth.

Once his tongue began to play, I was lost.

Lost in a world where I could think about nothing but Cooper and the bliss he was creating in my body.

"Yes," I whimpered as Cooper let go of my wrists and slipped his hands under my ass.

He sucked.

He nibbled.

He teased.

And then he satisfied.

I threaded my hands into his hair, avoiding his injuries, as I felt my climax building.

"Just make me come, Cooper," I pleaded. "You're killing me."

His tongue stroked over my clit and didn't back off this time.

Cooper gave me the pressure and seductive movement I needed to make my orgasm roll over me with so much strength that it left me gasping for breath.

"Yes. Please. That feels so good, Cooper. Please don't stop."

I lifted my hips to meet those wicked swipes of his tongue.

And then…I exploded.

I came long, hard, and screaming his name like it was my mantra. "Cooper! Cooper! Yes!"

My thighs were still trembling when Cooper started to kiss and lick his way up my body.

He stopped when he came to my breasts and gave them his undivided attention until I felt like I was going to pass out from pleasure.

He pinched.

He licked.

He nipped.

And then he soothed.

"If you don't stop teasing me right now I'm going to lose my mind," I said breathlessly.

Finally, he crawled up until he was eye to eye with me, his powerful body covering mine.

I wrapped my legs around his waist. "Fuck me, Cooper. Please. Now. I need you."

I yearned.

I ached.

I needed.

I wanted.

I craved.

All of those emotions revolved around the love and need that this man managed to wring out of my body every time he touched me.

I wrapped my arms around his neck and pulled him close, but it was as though I could never get close enough.

He put a hand behind my head and kissed me, devouring my mouth like he couldn't get close enough, either.

"I love you," I choked out when he finally released my mouth. "I love you so much, Cooper."

Those words made me vulnerable, but they also filled me with so much freedom that I felt like I could fly.

Cooper buried his face in my neck and tasted the skin there, knowing it drove me completely insane. "I love you, sweetheart. Tell me you'll never leave me."

A tear leaked from my eye as I realized that the newness of these emotions made both of us vulnerable. Since women had a habit of leaving him or not giving a damn about him, he was obviously as gob smacked as I was by the intensity of the emotions between us.

Hell, I felt just as exposed as he did, but ultimately, I trusted him, and I knew he trusted me, too.

"I'm never going to leave, Cooper. Ever. Maybe you've never believed in soul mates, but I do, and you're mine."

"You made me a believer," he said huskily as he buried his cock inside me. "There's only you, Torie. It's always been you."

I groaned and lifted my body up to plaster it against him, moving with him as he started to thrust into me over and over again.

As usual, I couldn't get close enough.

I wanted to climb inside this man until I was completely surrounded by him.

"Yes, Cooper. Fuck me. Harder," I begged.

He put a hand under my ass and yanked me against him as he surged into me.

That soothed some of my desire to get closer.

"Fuck, Torie, you feel so damn good," he said in a voice that was raw with emotion.

I stroked over his hair and finally sunk my nails into his back as I felt my orgasm getting closer.

"I fucking love it when you do that," he groaned as he started moving at an almost impossible speed.

I panted against his neck as my climax started to overwhelm me. "I can't wait any longer," I cried out.

"Don't wait, baby. Come for me," he demanded.

I did.

"Cooper!" I screamed as my body started to writhe underneath him. "I love you!"

I said that over and over just because I finally could.

"Fuck! I love you, too, baby," Cooper groaned as he found his own release.

He rolled and pulled me on top of him, but kept us joined as I fought for my breath and tried to slow my heart rate down.

"Are you okay?" I asked anxiously.

He chuckled as he kissed the top of my head. "Do you really have to ask that after what just happened?"

"Yes. You got your head bashed in and you still have a gazillion stitches, Cooper. Dammit! I thought maybe we could just take this one slow."

"Give it up, sweetheart," he said with humor in his tone. "Slow isn't happening anytime soon. And I'm okay with that. I'm just fine. We didn't have to slow it down. Not for me."

I let out a sigh as I made sure that putting my fingers in his hair hadn't messed anything up. "Your sutures look fine."

He grabbed my hand. "They are fine, baby. It would take a lot more than a little enthusiastic sex to pull those things out. They've been in for a while. The wounds are healing."

Cooper kissed my hand and then entwined our fingers and rested them on his chest as he added. "I missed you. You've been so standoffish for days now. I was tired of being a patient and not a boyfriend."

"Everything about this entire trip was scary," I told him. "This is the best part of the whole trip."

"Leaving?" he said with a grin.

I shook my head. "No. Being with you."

"Still sure you want to marry me?" he asked huskily.

"Do you really have to ask that after what just happened?" I asked, repeating his question. "I love you, Cooper Montgomery. I doubt you could become my husband fast enough."

"Oh, I could make it happen pretty fast," he argued. "Vegas in a month or so? Fuck! I know you deserve a big wedding with—"

"But that's not what I want," I told him. "Chase and Wyatt are really the only important family I have left, and it's not like I've had time or the opportunity to rebuild a network of friends in San Diego. If I had my way, I'd keep everything simple. Make it happen, Cooper. I'll figure out the best place to kidnap and take you to on our honeymoon."

I didn't want to wait, either. My biological clock wasn't ticking that loudly, but I was thirty-two, and if Cooper wanted kids like I did, we'd have to get that process moving in the next few years. "Do you want to have kids?" I asked hesitantly.

"With you? Hell, yes," he said without hesitation. "Well, if you want them. If you don't, I can live with that, too."

"I do," I told him softly as I stroked over his stubbled jaw. "I'd like to take a little time to be together first, though. Once we're settled and we've been able to travel a little together, I'll be ready. I've always wanted to have a child or two. I just wasn't sure if I'd ever meet the right guy."

He shot me a wicked grin. "I'm definitely at your service for that. No matter how long it takes."

I smiled back at him, my entire being filled with happiness.

"I wouldn't exactly be upset if it doesn't happen right away," he told me in a husky voice.

I laughed, my spirit light. "I'm so glad you're willing to practice until we get it right."

"Sweetheart, everything is right with me right now. I feel like the most fortunate bastard on Earth right now," he said earnestly.

I made a vow to make sure he always felt that way. No one deserved happiness, love, and laughter more than Cooper. After his childhood and his history with the women in his life, he deserved someone who would always love him, always appreciate all of the wonderful things about him.

"I'm feeling pretty lucky myself right now, handsome," I told him sincerely. "Nothing in my past matters anymore, Cooper, because in the end, I got you."

He frowned. "Considering what happened to you, that seems like a pretty lousy consolation prize."

I smacked him on the shoulder. "Stop that. You're the best of prizes."

He put a hand behind my head, pulled me close, and kissed me senseless before he said, "I'll always try to live up to that opinion."

"You already do," I told him softly as I lowered my head to kiss him again.

Cooper Montgomery might not realize it, but he was everything I'd always wanted, and I hadn't even needed to kiss another single frog to find him.

Epilogue

Torie

Three Months Later…

"Thank you both for not taking offense when I stepped in front of you in line to get married," I told Taylor and Harlow as we all sipped a glass of champagne in the enormous reception suite in Vegas.

As promised, Cooper had eagerly pulled a wedding together in Vegas. He took a little longer than initially promised so he could "make sure everything was perfect."

It had been.

Our small but beautiful ceremony had taken place in front of friends and family in a gorgeous chapel.

We'd kept the wedding formal without being stuffy.

I'd found an amazing tea-length, white lace dress that made me feel like a princess. I'd opted for a white, simple pearl and flower headpiece that was woven through my crazy hair rather than the traditional veil because it was more my style.

Savannah had stood up for me, and Chase had stood up for Cooper, which had taken the pressure off my husband of deciding which brother to use as a best man. It had allowed Hudson, Jax, Taylor, and Harlow to just be honored guests rather than going through the hassle of being part of a very small wedding party.

Our reception was being held in a fantastic penthouse suite with amazing food and plenty of space for our guests.

Everything about my wedding day had been absolutely splendid.

I glanced down at the flawless diamond ring that Cooper had slipped onto my finger soon after we'd returned from the Amazon. Of course, they were gems from the Montgomery mines, and the gigantic center stone had taken my breath away.

Cooper claimed he wanted to make sure every guy could see that I was taken.

I thought he was just continuing his trend of being the most amazing man on Earth.

Taylor snorted from her chair next to me. "Flying off to Vegas for a weekend on my fiancée's private jet wasn't exactly a hardship."

"Not for me, either," Harlow assured me from her seat on the other side of me. "And I don't blame you for not wanting to wait until after Jax and I get married next Valentine's Day. I think your wedding was perfect. I'm tempted to ask Jax if we can do the same thing."

"Do you think Riley is completely over the fact that her brothers lied to her about Last Hope?" I asked with a sigh.

Hudson, Jax, and Cooper had finally spilled the beans to their little sister about Last Hope about six weeks ago.

Riley had just started talking to them again two weeks ago, and probably only because of the wedding.

Cooper had been right. She had been upset, but she was currently talking with her brothers across the room like it had never happened.

"She's totally over it," Taylor assured me. "I think she was okay a week or two after they told her, but she wanted them to get the message that she wasn't okay with them telling all those stories about being treasure hunters."

I smiled. "I'm glad she knows. I'm always afraid I'll say something I shouldn't."

"Me, too," Taylor said in a relieved voice. "I hated having to watch everything I said when she was around. She's my friend."

"Mine, too," Harlow said as she smiled at me. "I heard we have you to thank for that."

I shook my head. "Not really. I just told Cooper what it's like to be a little sister. They made the decision to tell her."

Taylor let out a small sigh. "I can't believe you didn't tell us that Savannah Anderson is your best friend. She's so gorgeous, and she's such an amazing reporter. I'm not sure I'd be half as brave as she is about going into some of the world's hot spots."

I shrugged as I looked across the room at Savannah. "I guess I don't think of her as a celebrity. She's been my best friend since grade school, and being a journalist was always her dream. I've always been so proud of her, but I worry about her sometimes. I know she has security, but her job is still pretty dangerous."

"So what's the deal between her and Chase?" Harlow asked. "He can't seem to take his eyes off her. Are they an item?"

My gaze immediately flew to my best friend and my brothers, both of whom were at the buffet tables.

Savannah and Chase were having an animated conversation, which was nothing new.

I watched the two of them for a few minutes, but I didn't notice anything unusual.

"They're friends," I told Taylor and Harlow. "Savannah has always been the only female who could bring Chase down a peg or two. She never lets him get too cocky."

Harlow's gaze followed mine. "Maybe you're just used to the way Chase looks at Savannah like he wants to get her naked and devour her. Believe me, those looks are predatory."

"I have to agree," Taylor said. "The two of them look like they're friends or friendly acquaintances, but there's definitely some sexual tension there."

"No!" I denied. "Not those two."

Taylor raised a brow. "Maybe Savannah has never told you that she's hot for your brother because he's the dreaded brother of the best friend."

I rolled my eyes. "I think the whole idea of that being some kind of taboo is ridiculous. I've reminded Vanna that Chase and Wyatt are still single, and she's always refused like she had zero interest in either one of them. She's not holding back because he's my brother."

I continued to watch the two of them, trying to figure out if I'd been missing something.

I had to admit, Vanna's eyes were slightly wary even though she was smiling.

And Chase? Okay, maybe he was looking at Vanna a little differently from the way he used to when we were younger.

"Can you see what I mean?" Harlow asked quietly.

I nodded slowly. "I think you're right. God, how did I miss it? Something changed at some point during our friendship. I guess I just wasn't paying attention."

"I'm sure it happened after you were all grown-up," Harlow mused. "By that time, why would you even be looking? I think the only reason Taylor and I noticed is because we barely know Chase and we've never met Savannah. It was a lot more obvious. Do you think they'll ever figure out how they feel?"

"I'm not sure," I said thoughtfully. "They've known each other since they were kids, just like me and Vanna. They've always been a little antagonistic, but Chase was always just as protective of Vanna as he was of me as a child. He treated her like a second little sister."

"No offense," Taylor said. "But he's not looking at her like his little sister anymore."

"How much longer are you two planning on monopolizing my bride?" Cooper asked teasingly as he arrived from the buffet. "Hudson and Jax are starving, but they don't want to eat without you."

I accepted the plate that Cooper had filled for me from the table.

Taylor rose. "I'm ready to attack the food," she said with a laugh.

"Me, too," Harlow agreed as she got up. "We'll catch up with you a little later, Torie."

I waved at them as they went to find their fiancé's. Cooper quickly plopped into the chair that Harlow had vacated so he could start working on his own plate of food.

"How are you holding up?" Cooper asked.

I sighed. "I couldn't ask for a better wedding day. Thank you for the food. I'm starving."

I put my champagne glass down on the table in front of me so I could focus on my plate.

"How long before you think we can sneak out of here?" he asked as he devoured a huge helping of prime rib.

I nearly choked on my food. "Are you trying to sneak out of your own wedding? Our wedding?"

He nodded as he chewed and swallowed. "You're mine. I'm yours. Now I think we should get to reap the rewards."

I snorted. "This morning wasn't enough?"

He leaned over until his mouth was close to my ear. "It was, but then I saw you in that dress. Have I told you how beautiful you look today?"

"Several times," I reminded him. "Did I tell you how hot you look in a tux?"

He grinned. "Once or twice, but I don't mind hearing it again."

That mischievous smile of his was starting to make me wonder how soon we could escape, too.

"I love you, Cooper Montgomery. I'll remember today for the rest of my life."

I'd remember the confident way he'd said his vows.

The joy in his expression as I'd walked down the aisle.

And the promise of forever as I'd looked into his eyes.

He lifted his hand and palmed my cheek. "I'll make sure I remind you every single year on our anniversary. This date will never pass without me figuring out a way to celebrate my incredibly good fortune, sweetheart."

I sighed.

For a man who swore he wasn't romantic, he said some very sweet things.

"How much longer?" he said huskily.

"We haven't cut the cake yet," I reminded him. "And nobody is finished eating, not even my groom."

"You're right," he answered thoughtfully. "I'm not going to rush you. It's our wedding day."

My heart somersaulted. I knew how he felt.

We'd been so busy over the last few weeks getting ready for the wedding that I couldn't wait to have him all to myself and completely relaxed. "I can down a piece of cake pretty quickly," I teased. "And we can use our early departure for Europe in the morning as an excuse."

I had a fun hop around Europe planned for our honeymoon.

Cooper took my empty plate, dropped his on top of it, and put them on the small table next to him before he took my hand and raised it to his lips. "I love the way you think, Mrs. Montgomery."

"Do you?" I asked as I leaned toward him.

He nodded as he asked, "Do you have any idea how much I'm looking forward to starting our life together?"

My heart stuttered as I met his adoring gaze.

There would be more weddings in our future for our families.

There would be kids.

There would be laughter.

And I was sure there would be tears.

But I'd be facing the rest of my life with Cooper next to me, which was like a dream come true for me.

"I think I do know," I whispered. "Kiss me, Cooper."

He grinned as he swooped down to claim my lips, letting me know that he was more than ready to start that future together right that very minute.

~*The End*~

Author Note:

Even though I did take some creative license to make the Amazon pirates fit into this story, they actually are a thing. I first heard about river rats back in 2016 when pirates hijacked Delfin's Amazon Cruises' Amazon Discovery Cruise Ship. There were Peruvians, Americans, Australians, and two people from New Zealand on board. No one was killed, but the pirates made off with over $20,000 of passenger valuables. I can only imagine how frightening that had to have been for passengers. Although that was the first time I'd heard about the pirates, there had been other incidents on riverboat cruises prior to that incident. In 2014, one of the attacks by pirates led to the death of a passenger, and 7 passengers were injured. Barges that carry desirable cargo are probably one of the most at risk for piracy. These days, most riverboat cruises have plain clothed, armed security on the cruises. Barges and cargo boats are also utilizing security. It's a deterrent for pirates, but the piracy issue is far from being stamped out. As long as there are things to steal, I'm afraid that the river rats are probably there to stay.

Xoxo - Jan

Please visit me at:
http://www.authorjsscott.com
http://www.facebook.com/authorjsscott

You can write to me at
jsscott_author@hotmail.com

You can also tweet
@AuthorJSScott

Please sign up for my Newsletter for updates, new releases and exclusive excerpts.

Books by J. S. Scott:

Billionaire Obsession Series
The Billionaire's Obsession~Simon
Heart of the Billionaire
The Billionaire's Salvation
The Billionaire's Game
Billionaire Undone~Travis
Billionaire Unmasked~Jason
Billionaire Untamed~Tate
Billionaire Unbound~Chloe
Billionaire Undaunted~Zane
Billionaire Unknown~Blake
Billionaire Unveiled~Marcus
Billionaire Unloved~Jett
Billionaire Unwed~Zeke
Billionaire Unchallenged~Carter

Billionaire Unattainable~Mason
Billionaire Undercover~Hudson
Billionaire Unexpected~Jax

British Billionaires Series
Tell Me You're Mine
Tell Me I'm Yours

Sinclair Series
The Billionaire's Christmas
No Ordinary Billionaire
The Forbidden Billionaire
The Billionaire's Touch
The Billionaire's Voice
The Billionaire Takes All
The Billionaire's Secret
Only A Millionaire

Accidental Billionaires
Ensnared
Entangled
Enamored
Enchanted
Endeared

Walker Brothers Series
Release
Player
Damaged

The Sentinel Demons

The Sentinel Demons: The Complete Collection
A Dangerous Bargain
A Dangerous Hunger
A Dangerous Fury
A Dangerous Demon King

The Vampire Coalition Series

The Vampire Coalition: The Complete Collection
The Rough Mating of a Vampire (Prelude)
Ethan's Mate
Rory's Mate
Nathan's Mate
Liam's Mate
Daric's Mate

Changeling Encounters Series

Changeling Encounters: The Complete Collection
Mate Of The Werewolf
The Dangers Of Adopting A Werewolf
All I Want For Christmas Is A Werewolf

The Pleasures of His Punishment

The Pleasures of His Punishment: The Complete Collection
The Billionaire Next Door
The Millionaire and the Librarian
Riding with the Cop
Secret Desires of the Counselor
In Trouble with the Boss
Rough Ride with a Cowboy

Rough Day for the Teacher
A Forfeit for a Cowboy
Just what the Doctor Ordered
Wicked Romance of a Vampire

The Curve Collection: Big Girls and Bad Boys Series

The Curve Collection: The Complete Collection
The Curve Ball
The Beast Loves Curves
Curves by Design

Writing as Lane Parker

Dearest Stalker: Part 1
Dearest Stalker: A Complete Collection
A Christmas Dream
A Valentine's Dream
Lost: A Mountain Man Rescue Romance

A Dark Horse Novel w/ Cali MacKay

Bound
Hacked

Taken By A Trillionaire Series

Virgin for the Trillionaire by Ruth Cardello
Virgin for the Prince by J.S. Scott
Virgin to Conquer by Melody Anne
Prince Bryan: Taken By A Trillionaire

Other Titles

Well Played w/Ruth Cardello

Printed in Great Britain
by Amazon